TERMINUS

TALES OF THE BLACK
FANTASTIC FROM THE ATL

EDITED
BY
MILTON J. DAVIS

MVmedia, LLC
Fayetteville, GA

MVmedia, LLC
PO Box 1465
Fayetteville, GA 30214
www.mvmediaatl.com

Ordering Information:
Quantity sales. Special discounts are available on quantity purchases by corporations, associations, and others. For details, contact the "Special Sales Department" at the address above.

Terminus. -- 1st ed.
ISBN 978-0-9992789-2-5

Table of Contents

Bomani and the Case of the Missing Monsters

by

Balogun Ojetade

Well, this is a scary mess.

I wish I could say it was the scariest mess I've ever seen – *that* would belong to the *New Atlanta Child Murders* of 2009; kinda proved someone other than Wayne Williams did it back in '79 and is still out here – but this is certainly up there. Top five at least. The victim: Ricky Biggs, born August 21st, 1987. Just turned thirty years old, and apparently someone didn't want to wish him a very happy birthday. Actually, the vic' was born *Richard* Biggs, but he legally changed it to "Ricky" in '05. Guess being call "Dick Biggs" and you're not a porn star ain't no fun.

We find his legs – what's left of them – on the floor. It's like some kinda wild animal just chewed and chewed and then spit it all back out. There just ain't a lot left. The upper half of Ricky is still in the bed.

The vic' doesn't have the look, to me, of anyone who was ever handsome, but to be honest, I can't rightly judge a man whose eyes are hanging out of their sockets like smashed boiled eggs and whose face looks like someone – or something – decided to use it for a Tic Tac Toe board and a chainsaw to draw the x's and o's. I bring my face in closer – right up next to what's left of Ricky's mug and find two small holes in his neck. My eyes scan downward. Ricky's guts are drying out in the center of the bed; maggots are crawling slowly over them.

Goddamn, I have to back away! The stench is the worst. It's always the worst, but this is especially bad – like dirty ass on lemony fresh sheets. I pull out my handkerchief and cover my face. How long has he been rotting in here? Even the Atlanta late summer breeze can't cover this funk. You get used to the sights, but the smell? Even after thirty plus years of doing this, it's all I can do to hold down those spicy shrimp quesadillas from the *Flying Biscuit*. Should have known spicy shrimp quesadillas would be a bad choice.

"Man, partner… somebody really wanted this guy dead."

"Chewed up, spit out, and ripped in half? Yeah, Stitch, I'd say someone wanted ol' Ricky dead, and they wanted to make sure of it."

The lab rats'll take care of Ricky I'll come back later.

"C'mon Stitch. Let's get outta here."

* * *

With Ricky outta the picture, Stitch and I can roll up our sleeves and really get to the nitty-gritty. There are no signs of forced entry; the front door is locked. The apartment is on the third floor, but I check the windows anyway – nothing outta the ordinary.

The apartment itself is small, not like Midtown small, but it's not big. The pea soup green tiles in the kitchen and the lack of smelly soaps in the bathroom tell me that Ricky was living the bachelor's life. He seems to have kept it clean enough though. Not like neat-freak clean, but it's not dirty. Overall, it reminds me of a lot of places I used to have, back before I met Marisol… with one exception.

We all got our things. Me? I like to grab a cold bottle of good beer and paint those little pewter figurines from *Ki Khanga*, that African D-n-D-type game everybody's clamoring about on the internet nowadays. Mr. Ricky Biggs, on the other hand, his thing seems to be – or have been – scary movies. The whole place is a shrine to the eerie and weird. Not in like a 'serial killer' kind of way –

with the Atlanta Child Murderer still at large, Goddess knows we don't need another one of those. No, this is more in a 'fan of every spine-chilling movie you've ever seen, and then some' kind of way.

Take any psycho, slasher, evil alien, body-snatcher, zombie, or inbred cannibal you can think of and it's in here in at least one way or another. There are little figurines of creepy clowns, killer kids, and that guy with the needles in his ass. The walls aren't plaster or tile; they're VHS tapes. For real, Ricky? No DVDs? Not even a goddamn laser disc? I can't really trip, though. I still got *Best of the Isley Brothers* on cassette in my *Walkman* at home. The empty case of *Night of the Gnaw Maws* lies across the top row. I later find the tape sitting in the VCR. An old TV – even to *me* it's old – is playing nothing but fuzz, while some ghost stares at us from the rug on the floor. Two evil pumpkins watch me and Stitch's every move from the throw pillows. Shaquita, the Demented Drum Major, from that movie *I Know What Drumline You Killed Last Semester*, stares at me from the fleece blanket on the back of the couch. I hate how the eyes follow you around. Why do I even know who Shaquita is? Oh, because that's the one that Junior likes. Marisol says he's too young to be watching those types of things, but what good are grandpas if they can't spoil their grandkids?

"This guy sure did like his fright flicks, huh?"

"Looks like it, Stitch." Now, just because I know who Shaquita, the Demented Drum Major is, don't mean I know much about this spooky shit. "Stitch, I don't know half of this stuff, but take a look at this."

It seems that the cream-of-the-crop of Ricky's collection is his posters. The whole lot is very well maintained, but these posters just seem a little more, well… a little *more* maintained. The figurines and the tapes, they're all kind of just thrown together. But these posters, they take up space. Housed in polished wood frames and carefully hanged, these prints really bring the place together.

"Wow, *13 Magical Negroes*," Stitch says. "Classic!"

"You know this film?"

"Everybody knows *13 Magical Negroes*." Stitch stares at me like I'm from another planet. "It's a classic. Ya see, the doctor, Dr. Wingman, he starts doing these experiments on these Magical Negroes from popular films, television and fiction. The Magical Negroes, they start to develop a thirst for blood! Pretty soon, the Magical Negroes escape the lab and start attacking the city, while simultaneously saving white people *from* their attacks. It gets pretty wild from there."

"Ya know what… I think I have heard of that, Stitch." Now, I may not be 100% sure how scary a blood thirsty Magical Negro is, but I know when things don't add up. "Stitch, don't you think this poster looks a little... peculiar?"

Stitch stands a little closer, taking a hold of her thin glasses. Marisol tells me that Stitch needs to eat more, and she's right: The young woman looks like she'll keel over if she misses a meal. And I don't know how she sees anything but nostrils with those tiny eyes and that big nose, but she does good work. She's caught a few things I've missed in the past.

"Well," Stitch pondered.

It was a vintage style movie poster. *13 Magical Negroes* was written at the top, each letter dripping with horror font blood. A young Black woman in the corner, with her shirt ripped just enough to expose the bottom of one butterscotch-complexioned breast, stood with her hands up, protecting her face from some unseen terror.

"Well," Stitch starts again, "they certainly took some liberties with Gabrielle Beharie's boobs. They're not that big in real life."

"No Stitch," I sighed. "Look deeper." I scanned the poster. Other than the title and the woman with the big breasts, the poster is largely empty. I get so close to the poster, fog starts to form on the glass. Could be I'm looking too hard, but I swear there is a Magical Negro-sized fade in the picture.

"Wouldn't you think that a poster about Magical Negroes might have some Magical Negroes in it?"

Stitch nodded her head in acknowledgment. "Yeah, maybe so."

I walk over to the next poster: *Wulfpyr*. A full silver moon sits high in the poster, spotlighting an opening in the poorly drawn forest below, right where you might find a Wulfpyr – whatever the hell that is.

"*Wulfpyr*," Stitch says. "Pretty lame flick about the child of a Chinese werewolf and a Nigerian vampire.

Really only memorable because it's where Abiola Yee got her start."

"Abiola Yee started off as a scream queen?"

"Sure did."

"Huh." That's news to me. "Take a look here Stitch. Don't this look a little empty to you?"

"Yeah, I definitely think the artist could have made more use of the space."

"Me too, Stitch. Me too."

I walk around and check out a few more posters. *Day of the Living Volcano*: lots of lava and ash; a woman obviously not prepared for the next Pompeii and Mt. Vesuvius – but no Volcano. *Vampires Take Manhattan*: no vampires. *Ape-ocalypse*: ape free. And finally, *The Being* is being-less, unless the being is supposed to be invisible. Not so sure about that one.

"Stitch, grab these posters. Let's head down to the station."

* * *

The geeks in the lab tell me the official cause of death for Ricky was the removal of the inferior part of the body from the superior. So, much as I suspected, he was ripped in half. I wish I could say that I was surprised when they describe the rest of the injuries. Magical Negro scratches. Wulfpyr bites. The butter on the toast is when he hands me the gorilla's tooth.

"This guy one of those exotic animal collectors?" one of the geeks asks me.

"He was a collector all right."

"How in the hell did he get a Silverback all the way out here?" the other chimes in.

"It's Atlanta," I say with a shrug. No more explanation needed.

Now, in most cities and towns around the country, some poor nobody with a bent for scary movies gets ripped apart by a zoo full of animals, this would be big news. But Atlanta ain't most cities. This city's been strange since old Widow Goodweather stole the recipe for shrimp-n-grits from the Muskogee Native Americans some three hundred odd years ago.

Nobody really knows – or at least *I* don't really know, and that's good enough for me – why Widow Goodweather left Chi-town to strike out on her own. And nobody really knows why she chose to plant her new roots right here in Atlanta, either. Couldn't have been for the ocean view. But, for whatever reason, she did, and she stole from her Muskogee neighbors and now, grits are the official food of Georgia and *shrimp*-n-grits is the official food of Atlanta.

The ghost story goes that she made a deal with some ungodly types, and in return she got her own university where she could experiment on grits the way George Washington carver experimented on the peanut. The school grew unnaturally quickly in prominence and, to this day, young men and women come from all over the world to learn, study, and perhaps get a glimpse of the place's...eh, let's call it *strange*...history. Now what Widow Goodweather – the woman – did *exactly*, I can't tell you. And what goes on now, well, some of it I *still* can't tell you, and, the other parts, I *wish* I couldn't tell you. But I can tell you we can thank Widow Goodweather for shrimp-n-grits, fish-n-grits, cheese grits and sugar grits. Really, we could thank the Native American, but we always give the credit for the contributions of Native Americans to someone else. It's the American way.

So, to say that Ricky's death was unusual, well, it was… and it wasn't.

"There's one more thing." The geek in the lab coat hands me a small, partially chewed up piece of paper. "Not sure how that thing made it intact."

I uncrumple the paper and hold it up to the light. Through the blood, I can barely make out the writing: *Papa Morte's Bazaar Bizarre of Creepy Collections.*

I grab Stitch and decide to pay Papa Morte a visit.

* * *

On the way over Stitch tells me that, much like the Silverback tooth in my pocket, those posters we found back at Ricky's are very real… with one minor anomaly:

"Not only are they real," Stitch tells me, "they're originals. Not those cheap prints you can just order anywhere."

"Is that so?"

"That's so," Stitch continues. "The thing is... the originals should have the monster in the poster."

"I imagine they should, Stitch."

I pull into the parking lot. *Papa Morte's Bazaar Bizarre of Creepy Collections* sits in a strip mall, right off of I-285, stuck between a *Starbucks* and the *Afrikan Martial Arts Institute*. A group of 4-6-year olds throw knee and elbow strikes in unison like a tiny little army in training. I must have grabbed a cup o' Joe at that Starbucks a hundred times – sometimes I'll order a vanilla chai latte, when I'm feelin' sophisticated – but, in all my years in the ATL, I don't remember ever seeing Papa Morte, nor his 'bizarre bazaar'.

The bell rings as Stitch and I walk through the door to Papa Morte's. I might have expected a mysterious old man in a cramped room full of incense and monkey skulls. Instead, I get a fat kid with thick glasses behind the counter and a room full of anything you can put an undead face on. They got alien egg ice cube trays, sexy witch lighters, even Shaquita the Demented Drum Major has a few action figures to play with. Comic books, games, and of course movie posters line the walls. At a table in the back, a few more fat guys with thick glasses sit around a table, hunched over some dice and cards.

"I told you, my sparkly zombie with the machete kills your yoga instructor with the healthy snacks."

"No, you forgot to add plus two because my yoga instructor's chakras are in alignment!"

I leave the guys in the back. I like RPGs, but yoga instructors are just too weird for me.

"You Papa Morte?" I ask the kid behind the counter, knowing the answer. He's not old enough to be a Houngan.

"Me? No, I'm Roger." He puts down his book and pushes his glasses back. "What can I do you for?"

"You familiar with a Ricky Biggs, Roger?" I hold up a picture of a fully together Ricky to refresh Roger's memory.

"Ricky? Oh yeah. Comes in here all the time." Roger looks at me and Stitch. "What happened?"

"Someone decided they got tired of seeing Ricky in one piece," Stitch says.

"Thought he looked better as a two piece," I add.

"What? Are you—" Roger looks from Stitch to me. We nod. "Oh my god."

I pull out the receipt. "We found this in his pocket."

"Wow, uh yeah," Roger pulls himself together. "He was just in here a couple days ago. He picked up that *Being* poster."

"That would be the original 81 x 81 inch *The Being* movie poster issued by Spector Brothers Studio in 1954?"

"That's the one. A real beaut," Roger tells us. "Ricky had been looking for that one for a long time."

"Ricky," I ask. "He bought a lot of these posters from you?"

"Well, a lot of everything really," Roger informs me. "Comics, collectible figures, lighters, magnets, pillows. Anything that had anything with a horror movie, he wanted it. But, yeah, he especially loved these posters."

"Any reason why he was so into these flicks?" Stitch is really working for her pay today.

"Why does anyone like anything?" Roger replies. "I guess he just liked being scared. The guy didn't seem to have a lot of friends or anything. Not that he was like one of those weirdo loner types. I mean, he was kinda strange, but not in a bad way. But then who out here isn't kinda strange?"

I have to agree. "You got that right, Roger."

"I mean, he came in here all the time and we'd chat every once in a while, about some new movie or he'd ask me to order something for him."

"Like these posters?"

"Yeah, he was very meticulous about the posters. They had to be original. Like HAD to be. Ricky loved to collect his stuff, but most of it, he wasn't too particular about. Those posters though? He knew what he wanted."

"And you have these posters here?"

"Well, we have prints," Roger says. "But not originals. We have a guy for the originals."

"A guy?"

"Wi, Detectif." A new voice enters the conversation. "Yon nèg afich. How you say? A poster guy."

I turn to find myself face to chest with an unusually tall man. I'm six-one, but this brother makes me look like a toddler. But he's thin – skinnier than a mumble rapper's jeans. Probably one of those raw vegan, shea butter soldier-types. Even though he's incredibly thin, he's cleaner than hand sanitizer. Impeccable. A watch chain shines from the button on his vest. A pencil thin mustache moves with every syllable he speaks.

"Papa Morte, I presume?"

* * *

Papa Morte leads Stitch and me past the gamers into a tiny backroom. Incense instantly fills my nose. A monkey skull sits on a desk, surrounded by a collection of other tiny skulls, bones, and animals in jars full of fluid. Books line the walls, written in languages that I didn't even know existed. On the opposite wall, a collection of figurines pile upon a shelf. One figurine has the body of a man and the head of an octopus with tentacles falling from where the mouth should be. A set of figurines has a woman with a large headwrap ripping out the guts of a shirtless man. Jewelry, candles, and other talismans fill every single inch of free space. Clearly, we've now found the good stuff.

Papa Morte sits behind the desk with the monkey skull. I suck in my gut so as not to knock anything over. Stitch taps me on the shoulder. She nods at the wall above the good houngan's seat.

Just above the tall man's head is a poster. The moonlight. The swamp. The title. I've seen this before. At least, I've seen most of it. The only difference is that smack in the middle of this one stands a tall, pale, scaly thing with glowing eyes, fangs that'll rip your neck out and claws that'll cut through human flesh like a Ginsu knife through steel cans. It's *The Being*.

"You're a fan too huh?" I ask the houngan.

"Much like Mr. Biggs," Papa Morte steeples his hands in front of his face, "I am a collector." I swear I can hear the words slide over his tongue.

"How do you know Mr. Biggs?" Stitch asks.

"He and I did business together several times. As I said, we are both collectors," Papa Morte leans back. "Kindred spirits."

"He *was* a collector," I correct. "He's dead now."

"Unfortunate," Papa Morte says with a tone that implies it's not unfortunate at all. Or maybe I'm just hearing things.

"Yes, very," I say. "He won't be able to ride any of the rides at *Six Flags*. He's too short now… both halves of him."

"That's too bad," Papa Morte strokes the monkey skull as if it was still a monkey. "It's so rare to meet anyone who appreciates the fine arts as much as he did."

"He certainly seemed to like his horror movies," Stitch says.

"Yes," the houngan agrees. "But what he especially appreciated was the quality of the classics – the emotion;

the feeling of a fear… not the cheap thrills, not the gore of these films today… if we can even call them films."

"Well, someone certainly appreciated the gore," I say. "He was ripped in two and chewed up. Not a lot of quality in that."

Papa Morte looks unmoved.

"He actually has that same poster in his room." Stitch points up to *The Being.* "Well, almost the same."

"Of course, he does. I procured it for him," the houngan volunteers. "As well he should. Any serious collector should have a work of this... caliber. He's only fortunate that I could find a second."

"So, this *Being*, it's rare?"

"Extremely. Only a handful exists, and I was lucky enough to come across two."

"Lucky you," I say.

Papa Morte lets go half a smile.

"The only difference between his and yours," I say, stepping closer to Papa Morte, "is that his don't have no being in it."

"That must make it extra rare." Stitch matches my tone.

The Vodou priest looks to Stitch, completely ignoring me. "A misprint on this poster would, indeed, be extremely rare. And valuable." Papa Morte looks toward me. "But that's not the case. The poster I sold is an original, 1954 *The Being* print. I inspected it myself before selling it to Mr. Biggs. In fact, I considered trading mine with his, so exceptional was the print. But I just knew I couldn't live with myself if I did something so heinous."

"Who could?" I say, matching his gaze. "But, regardless, Ricky's print is now being-less."

Papa Morte offers us a look of non-explanation.

"When did you sell Ricky this picture?"

"As you know, three days ago." That *is* what the receipt said.

"Was there anything unusual about Ricky at that time?" I ask.

"Not at that time, no."

"At another time?" Stitch picks up on Papa Morte's word choice.

"There was a problem with Mr. Biggs's payment going through. The problem was, and is, that it *didn't* go through."

"The payment didn't clear?" Stitch asks.

"No; and now it seems that the poster has been defaced as well." Papa Morte looks away and then back at us. "All of this in addition to the grisly details of Mr. Biggs' death. Bondye mwen! This *is* a mess."

"It certainly is, Papa." I put my hands on the desk. "Did you and Ricky have any sort of discussion about this payment?"

This time, the doctor meets my gaze. "I called to tell him that there was a problem with the payment. He assured me that he would check into it and clear the whole thing up right away. I have worked with him several times in the past, always without incident, so I simply chalked the whole thing up to a bank error or a misunderstanding of some sort." The priest pauses. "Though, it was for quite a sum of money."

"How much we talking, Papa?" Stitch asks.

The houngan tells us.

"That's a lot of cheddar," I say.

"Wi, li se, detective." Papa Morte's fingers glide over the monkey skull, as his eyes do the same thing over my face. He's looking for something, but I closed myself up to his type long ago.

"So, Papa Morte," I meet his gaze. "Are you a houngan part-time and a procurer of rarities the rest of it?"

"I'm also a student," Papa Morte replied. "A Ph.D. candidate, actually." He stands, towering above me. "From Clark-Atlanta University. In History. Ancient African History."

"Quite a leap from Ancient African History to Modern American Cinema." Stitch is playing with one of the figurines from the shelf. It's the woman and her human sacrifice.

"Don't touch that please." Papa Morte walks out from behind his desk. "And not such a leap. The stories we tell today are not so different from the stories told thousands of years ago. Only now," the houngan takes the figurine out of Stitch's hand and places it gently back on the shelf, "we watch the horrors on the big screen or on TV, instead of in real life."

I'm not so sure about that. "Sure Papa. We'll be in touch."

* * *

I drop Stitch off back at the station.

"Creepy, huh?" Stitch tries to hold back a shudder. "That guy makes me feel like an ant under a magnifying glass."

"Welcome to Atlanta, sis." But Stitch is right; something don't add up about that guy. He was holding out on us for sure. "Get some rest Stitch. We'll figure this out tomorrow."

A chill engulfs my body as Stitch opens the car door. It's gotten cold. In August? Stitch shuffles over to her ride. I put mine in drive and head home.

* * *

I sit in the dark and watch as cold rain comes down like a silver sheet over the city. In the last few hours, it seems to have changed seasons. The day, like my bones, has gotten much too cold. This case, though, I won't let that go cold. The good houngan wasn't telling us everything, but then, what exactly was he hiding? Is he the kind of guy who would rip a man in half over a movie poster?

Yeah, I'd say he is.

I swirl the last swallow of Jackie D and Cola in my glass then gulp it down. It does nothing to warm my belly. Marisol has long since gone to bed, and I should join her. I've spent too many nights sleeping in this chair, dreaming of catching bad guys. Tonight, I haven't even taken my Sig off my waist.

I stand up and start to walk towards the stairs when the sound of running water catches my ear. I must have always heard it, the sound blending into the background. How long has it been going? It's not like Marisol to leave the sink running.

Oh, what in the—

My socks instantly become sopping wet as I enter the kitchen. The running water has overflowed the sink, and now I'm toe deep in water.

"Shit!" I look into the sink. It's dark, but there's something clogging up the drain. If it ain't one thing it's another.

I reach down and start feeling around. Something clammy and scaly, brushes against my palm. Did Marisol have fish for dinner? Ow! I feel my finger drag over one of the scales as I pull my hand back. There's a pretty nice cut on my index finger. Good job, old man.

I put the finger up to my mouth to try to stop the bleeding. It looks like I'll live. I stick my left hand down into the water this time, trying to be more careful this time.

I feel the fish scales again, right over the drain, but for whatever reason, I can't pull it out.

I feel around some more. The water is thick, almost sludgy, over my arm. Looks like we'll have to get this checked out too. Suddenly, I don't have to find the fish guts anymore. They've found me.

Like a thousand little bullets, something clamps down on my arm. I feel my skin, muscle, bone, flesh being ripped away. Then another something clamps down and I feel it all over again. And again. I pull my arm back.

Blood. Bone. Stump.

Stupid, old man.

Out of the darkness of the water, something jumps up at me. About a foot long. Scaly. The moonlight catches the tip of the dorsal fin and rows of razor sharp teeth.

I don't think. With my one good hand, I just punch the little shark in its face.

It goes flying back into the sink.

I've never been accused of being the smartest knife on the rack, but I stick my face over the sink to see about half a dozen miniature sharks fighting over the remains of what used to be my left hand. One notices me and takes a flying leap for my face. This time I swing my stump, sending blood flying, as I knock that death machine back into the water. It's not getting my good hand... or my pretty face.

Speaking of good hands and knives, I use the one to grab the other out of the knife block next to the sink, and I start stabbing wildly. Blood. Water. Shark guts. Pieces of my arm. They all go flying. This ain't the first time I've had to stab something under water, and it probably won't be the last.

I don't know how long this goes on, but I stop swinging when the sink is a stew of blood and fish brain. I stop to catch my breath, and I hear a splash of water behind me. Did one of those buggers slip by me?

I turn around to see something behind me, but this ain't no shark. It's tall, pale, and scaly. It's got glowing eyes, fangs that'll rip out my neck, and claws that'll cut through what's left of my flesh like one of those late night Ginsu knives through steel cans. It's the thing from that poster, *The Being*. Well, at least I've found him. It squats a bit, grunts and something falls from between its scaly legs – another shark; pooped onto the floor by this being. The shark flops around madly, trying to wiggle toward me.

I decide I'd rather bring a gun to this knife fight. I throw down the blade then draw my Sig. I fire once and hit the thing right between the eyes. It keeps coming, faster now. I fire again. And again. And again. I empty all eight shots into its face before it finally falls down. The Being is dead. In my kitchen.

"Bomani?" I hear Marisol's voice from upstairs. "Everything ok down there?"

"Yes, dear." I kick the Being in the head for good measure. "Just cleaning up the kitchen."

* * *

The snow has stopped falling, and the sun is just coming up as I pull off I-285 and into the strip mall. The docs fixed me up real good. Looks like I'll have to give up my dream of being a famous violinist, but I can still shake hands, and I can still shoot. And I can choke the shit out of Papa Morte.

I may not be able to pee in a urinal and text at the same time no more, but I found out I still came out better than Stitch. The guys tell me that they found her doing her best Ricky Biggs impression. Half of her they found inside her apartment. The other half outside, beside a set of large, ape-like footprints.

Anywhere else, they would have locked me in the nuthouse when I told them my story. But this is Atlanta. They've started searching for the Silverback.

No one – not my buddies on the force, not the docs, not Marisol – is thrilled about me heading out to pay a visit to Papa Morte, but I go anyway. The parking lot is empty, save for a couple early risers looking for their cup of mud over at the *Starbucks*. No one is kicking or punching at the *Afrikan Martial Arts Institute*. I pull right up to the curb then storm out.

I walk up to the front door of *Papa Morte's Bazaar Bizarre of Creepy Collections* and bear down on that front door like it's my job to open it, but it don't budge. I bang on the door with my good hand.

“Papa Morte! Open up!” In all my rage, it takes me a minute before I see the “For Lease” sign hanging right in front of my face. I get right up next to the glass and look in. Empty.

Just yesterday, that room was full of every type of horror you could think of. A group of nerds in the back. Roger at the front counter. Now… all gone; completely empty.

I step back to see the “Commercial Property! Call 812-555-6667” sign. I look to my left: *Starbucks*. To my right: the Afrikan Martial Arts Institute. This *is* the right place. I look in again. I can see the door in the back that leads to the cramped office of Papa Morte. I can only imagine that is empty as well.

“Damn it!” I kick the bottom of the front door. “Shit!” Now I have a stump for an arm AND a broken toe.

An old lady gives me a side-eye as she heads in for coffee. I hobble back to my car then head out.

* * *

We never find the Silverback that ripped Stitch and, I presume, Ricky in half. And somewhere between my home and the morgue, the bodies of that shark apocalypse and the Being are forever lost. I try to dig a little deeper. No records of anyone ever named Morte earning a history doctorate at Clark-Atlanta University. There aren’t even any records of the *Bazaar Bizarre of Creepy*

Collections ever being registered in the strip mall. The website, the phone book listing – all have just vanished like they never existed.

But the bodies of Ricky Biggs and Karen L. Bostitch – "Stitch" – have not disappeared. They're still in the ground at Oakland Cemetery. My left arm is still a stump, and I'm still here, with APD Homicide, where the unusual is too usual.

I still do some internet searches for "Papa Morte" or *13 Magical Negroes* or *The Being*. But just as the good houngan told me, those originals are hard to come by.

Sometimes, I find something interesting. Like this morning, on E-Bay, I came across a rare 1954 original poster. The glowing eyes. The fangs. The Ginsu claws. It's *The Being* in all its glory. I felt my heart start to beat a little faster as I read the ad below it:

ALL ORIGINAL CLASSIC MONSTER MOVIE POSTERS!

THE BEING! DAY OF THE LIVING VOLCANO! WULFPYR! AND MORE!!

BEST PRICES! CALL TODAY! 100% ORIGINAL!

PAPA MORTE'S BAFFLING BOTANICA (AND OTHER NEAT KNICK-KNACKS!)

666-555-1979

I think I will call today.

Play the Wraith

By

Azziza Sphinx

Traveling through veils is not supposed to be like this. One step through and we hit the other side. No funky time travel. No ominous emptiness. Just in and out. So, when an unexpected slap of power hit me, I knew something was wrong; someone had tampered with this veil, someone who didn't want us following. The air siphoned from my lungs. My body shut down as my brain prioritized the limited supply of oxygen. Next, cold crept in, my limbs growing heavy then hot before the prickling of cell death seized my insides.

The sensation of falling, the rushing of air and time spiraling by eased the panic moments before darkness pulled me under. My back smacking against something solid snatched me back from the abyss. That and the searing pain radiating through every limb. I wasn't sure if it was from the cold, or the damage done from the impact. Through the haze in my mind and blurred vision, I made out an expanse of tombstones stretching out before me.

A sizzle followed. Waves of heat caressed my skin, drawing me in. I rolled away just as the energy crackled, the place above where my head once was tearing before spitting out my partner like a discarded watermelon seed. He plinked against the white marble headstone adorned with cherub like angelic faces.

The debilitating pain forced my body into the fetal position.

"Clyde. Clyde wake up."

He grumbled, nearly inaudible had it not been for my Wraith hearing.

"Clyde, I think I'm really hurt over here."

He shot up, the green glow of his scythe bathing us in shadows. His eyes searched the surrounding area for potential dangers before they came to rest on me. I saw the pity there, the, '*if I hadn't been a girl, I would have thought to turn before allowing the force of descent to splatter me across the ground.*' It only lasted a split second before he banished his scythe and dropped to the ground beside me.

"Where does it hurt?"

Really? I'm lying here curled over like an infant, tears streaming from my eyes. Where the hell do you think it doesn't hurt?

"Everywhere."

He reached for me, and I cringed.

"I have to check. This may be' --he paused, searching for the least frightful response-- "uncomfortable."

I almost blacked out as his hand raced over my body. His touch was gentle; his way of either trying to make the task less painful or fear that pressing too hard might exasperate the injuries.

"Can you feel this?"

He moved to the extremities, starting with the fingers he pried from a fisted position.

"Yeah. Tingling but I can feel it."

"And this?"

Hot white pain shot up my side as his fingers traveled down my left leg. I couldn't hide the agony, though I had been trained to do so. I resorted to grunting so loud it drew his attention to our surroundings to make sure no one discovered us. I'd been through worse collecting rogue reapers. Getting beat up came with the job of being a Wraith – a rogue Reaper collector. I was sure I'd experience this pain again. Still, I hoped the beating of pain into my body over the years hardened my resolve or at least made these situations more bearable. Unfortunately, this wasn't proving to be true.

"Guess that answers my question," Clyde said. "I suppose there's no need to ask you to try to move."

"I can if you need me too." If danger lurked nearby, I'd do what I had to do. "Won't promise not to scream though."

"Don't."

Thankful for his response I remained as still as possible, taking shallow breaths to reduce the imaginary knives stabbing at my insides. I loathed being vulnerable like this. As a Wraith, my job was to take down the bad guys, rogue Reapers, which meant I needed to keep in tip top shape. Yet, here I lay, as defenseless as a newborn bunny, at the mercy of my enemy and the Universe.

"Drink."

Clyde shoved a straw in my face, my lips wrapping around the yellow and white plastic as I inhaled the healing liquid. It too came with a price. When the last drop passed my tongue, a rough hand slapped across my mouth. My body arched, rearing up as every cell came to life, regenerating and repairing the damage. A massive body slammed into mine, and I realize Clyde was on top of me, his attempt to keep me quiet while reducing the potential of me hurting myself.

My head rolled to the side, eyes locking on the sun shining in the grass, the image turning hazy as they glazed over. I don't recall blinking as shock set in. Only the change in the shadows, the repositioning of light to dark told me at least a few hours had passed before my mind and body returned to sync.

"What happened?" I managed as I slowly sat up.

"You were hurt pretty bad."

"Not that. I remember that part. I mean the veil." I wiggled my fingers and then my toes, making sure everything functioned correctly before moving to bigger areas such as my legs.

"I'm not sure."

"What do you mean you're not sure? You're the expert. Did The Book say anything…"?

"Whoa. Slow down."

He tossed me a sandwich, my stomach reminding me I was due for nourishment. While the tea of the Nai healed my body, it took a lot out of me. I'd need at least two heavy meals to combat the effects of the process.

"Sorry. I'm a bit out of it."

"Understood. I haven't had the opportunity to reference The Book. Priorities you know."

I did. I knew exactly what he meant. Clyde always kept the book near, stashed away in a secure pocket. It held Reaper and Wraith history: from the moment Death broke the rules to create us to the moments before we dropped into this world. New pages appeared each day, relevant facts and tidbits to pass on to generations to come.

But I couldn't lose sight of our purpose. We came here to wrangle a rogue Reaper – a time stealer. A special place in the Sands of Time awaited those who stole time from others. That was our mission, to bring justice, and hopefully, peace, to souls snatched from their timelines too soon. However, to do our jobs, we too needed to stay alive and unnoticed for as long as possible.

"So now what?"

"We wait."

"We wait? What do you mean we wait? Where the hell are we anyway?"

"Graveyard."

"No shit Sherlock. You know what I mean."

He huffed before filling me in. "The sign out front says Westview Cemetery."

"And exactly how do you know this?" I know he didn't leave me here to look for signage.

"Slow down. I know what you're thinking, but that's not what happened. I overheard a conversation from a couple looking for their ancestors."

A likely story. My gaze drifted to the Gothic Style Mausoleum a few rows in front of us, the six archways like gaping mouths preparing to swallow up souls. I'd say this place was quiet, but not in the traditional sense. I could see traffic zooming by on the streets outside of the gates. And yes, that attributed to the busy-ness of the location. But to tell the truth, the voices vied for my attention. Whispers among those in mourning paired with those mourned created a cacophony that made my head ache.

"Lavenia."

The whisper of my name made my blood run cold. My stomach dropped, the pounding in my chest making my ribs hurt. I dared not take a breath for fear of discovery. I don't like when things murmur in my head. Those voices usually lead to bad things to come.

"We should get inside," Clyde said.

I detected the faintest glow from his fingers, an impending signal of danger on the horizon. I felt it too, someone or something stalking in the distance. Maybe it was our rogue Reaper. Or maybe it was something else. Something much darker and terrifying, something that even as Wraiths we heeded and avoided.

"Let's go," I said, quickly getting to my feet.

We moved through the graves, careful to stick behind the bigger tombstones, weaving in a zigzag pattern separating at some places and coming together at others. Luckily this side of the cemetery was empty, so we managed to slither into the Abbey unnoticed. We found an inconspicuous spot to hunker down and waited.

I must have drifted off to sleep at some point because I woke to Clyde calling my name, gently shaking my shoulder to arouse me from the land of the sand man.

"What?"

"Our ride is here."

Though it was still early, the sun had retreated, leaving only the artificial illumination from the streetlights lining the road. A light mist hung in the air as we eased from our hiding place. The temperature had dropped as well, and we added a layer of clothing before daring to venture out to the graves.

"Where exactly is this ride?"

Clyde cut his eye in my direction. "I never said it was right outside the door. We need to make it to the front gate and across the street."

I followed his lead as we dashed through the tombstones and over the graves with copper markers secured in the ground. He made it sound so easy I was a bit taken aback when we reached the front gate to find them locked.

"Dammit. We're later than I thought."

"Now what?"

The look he shot my way was like a slap in the face. "On no." I staggered back in disbelief at the silent suggestion. "Not after what happened the last time."

"Oh, come on. You can't live in fear."

"Last time I checked, we weren't living at all." Okay, maybe the last comment was uncalled for; didn't change my mind though.

"Suit yourself. Stay here if you like. But we have reservations and one stop to make."

His scythe materialized, and without a moment of hesitation, he sliced through his hand. A second later, he stood on the other side of the gate.

"Uh. Fine." I did the same, a mini veil appearing before me when the first drop of Wraith blood bubbled to the surface.

A tickling sensation brushed across my skin, a hand reaching out, seizing my palm dragging me away from the veil. I turned to find… nothing. No ghostly figure, no haunting entity. I was on the ground then, fingers squeezing around my neck. I couldn't breathe, couldn't scream as my nails dug into the invisible something sucking the life out of me.

Then, just as quickly as it came, it was gone. I was on my back, gasping for air, the moon bathing my face in luminescence. Refusing to play victim any longer than necessary I summoned my scythe and sliced through the atmosphere conjuring a gateway using not my power as Wraith, but that of the High Priestess of the Nai. My confidence restored, considering I maintained full control over this entryway to the other side, I stepped through with the faint echo of a slurp and with a final smack it closed behind me.

Clyde didn't say a word as I slid onto the seat next to him. Was it possible he hadn't seen what happened? Maybe he was hiding something? I didn't recognize the man behind the wheel, so maybe he was playing it cool until we could talk in private.

"You know this guy?" I whispered as we pulled on to I-20 heading east.

"Lyft."

"What?"

He pulled a phone from his pocket, opening one of the applications and shoving the contraption in my face.

"My dear country girl. See. It's a driving service." Clyde appears older than me. He likes to call me country girl when I don't ‘get’ something new, especially technology. Keeps people from asking too many questions.

"Like a taxi?" I was familiar with taxis. Even private limo companies but this Lyft thing was new.

"Yes and no. From what I gather, there are fewer regulations. And a lot more flexibility. Instead of calling a company, requesting a ride then having to wait, this allows you to put the request out there, and the closest driver can accept. The destination is pre-programmed, and payments are online, which means no need for carrying cash."

Interesting. Our driver's name was Josh. He offered us bottled water of which I accepted, and Clyde declined. I stared out the window watching the traffic and a little of the city as we merged onto I-75. We reached the Hyatt Regency in fifteen minutes, the lights on Peachtree deciding to play more red light than green. I followed him through the glass doors as we headed to the concierge's desk.

"This is where we're staying?" I asked. Clyde typically preferred quieter places, off the beaten path. A hotel smack dab in the center of the bustling city was so not his M.O.

"No, but we may need a place close if this takes longer than expected. Or at least until we can acquire private transportation. I also thought you might want to freshen up before our evening meeting."

"Oh, I have time for that? What happened to 'we have reservations?'?"

"We do, but I know how you are, so I allotted a buffer just in case. Besides, our associate isn't scheduled to join us until nine. So, you have an hour."

I milled around the lobby as Clyde checked in. The place was comfortable. Not as busy as I expected, though I supposed considering we were checking in during dinner hours people were probably already out. A little girl in a pink dress waved at me. Her mother took one look in my direction and quickly ushered her too friendly off-spring in another direction. The disdain in the woman's face made me self-conscious.

I tapped Clyde on the shoulder. "I'm going to the re-stroom."

"No need--he handed me a key card--you can go to the room. I'll be up in a few."

I took full advantage of my allocated time, spending most of it in the shower. I managed to keep my back to the mirror as I dried off. Me and mirrors hadn't seen eye to eye in a long time. I saw things in them, unnatural things. So, I avoided them. Period. End of Story.

Clyde was flipping through channels when I exited the bathroom. He'd changed into slacks and a dress shirt, his dark hair freshly combed. He'd softened his features-a trick Nero taught each member of his ban of misfits-appearing less intimidating though he still held an edge about him.

"I know you're not a fan of dresses so I did what I could."

We'd shared the same house for decades; he was one of the few people my lover trusted with my life. I was precious cargo to all of my body guards, and not just be-cause Death was my bedmate. Though I didn't know all of the details, apparently somewhere in a former life I'd sacrificed myself to save the universe. My payment, be-ing bound to Death as a reminder for him to not break "the rules" again. It wasn't all bad: immortality and all. The only downside was when Death's list called, we collected. Sometimes it was easy. Most times it wasn't. But it kept life interesting.

I pulled the rust colored jumper from the bag tossed over one of the beds. It was the perfect color, a contrast to my dark skin. A smaller bag dropped out when I slid the plastic all the way over. Inside, matching bangle with yellow and brown highlights and a pair of handcrafted earrings.

"You shouldn't have."

"Oh, I didn't."

I didn't want to know. Or…well…I already knew so I dropped it. "I'll be ready in five."

Indifferent, he let me go dress without another word. Another of those ride shares and twenty minutes and the hostess showed us to our table. I liked the place, the southwestern motif intriguing. The sign out front read Agave, and the smells engulfed me the minute we stepped in the door. It was a comfortable, cozy atmosphere, shots of tequila flying by while servers and patrons vied for prime real estate. Across the street, a stone wall stood as a measly divider between the restaurant and the final resting place of some of the city's most influential families.

Since Clyde knew who it was that we were scheduled to rendezvous with, I chose to sit with my back to the door giving him a perfect view of those coming and going. Besides, I'd had enough of cemeteries to last me a lifetime and then some.

Settled in, Clyde ordered each of us a shot and requested a little time to review the menu.

"So, who are we meeting?" I asked as I perused the offerings. So many choices and everything sounded great. I eventually decided on the Spicy Tequila Anejo Shrimp while Clyde flatly refused to provide any additional information regarding our meeting.

I suspected this resource would provide us additional information about our rogue Reaper. We had little at this point. An hourglass Clyde kept close indicated that a Reaper's time had run out and it was up to us to return him or her to the Sands from which we came. Otherwise, no dossier. No definitive answers. Just the initial pull leading us to Atlanta. But Clyde kept contacts all over the world. Some from the previous life of a body he temporarily inhabited and others from devilish dealings. As he once told me, in his original lifetime he was a "very very bad man," and I believed some of that stayed with him, which is why Nero honored him with the highest level of power granted to those who walked between the worlds.

Old power seeped into my bones as I took the last bite of my shrimp. No other patrons appeared to notice as a whoosh of air sent goose bumps up my arms. Clyde downed his third shot as impending doom drew closer. With my back to the door, I watched as a shadow approached. The seat next to mine slid out, and a dark-skinned man with a shaved head wearing a necklace of bones plopped down next to me. He kept his eye facing forward, the scar on his right cheek deepening as he chewed on a stick of what smelled like ginger.

I don't know what I expected, but it wasn't the otherwise well-dressed gentleman who could pass for a hit man had it not been for the deadly neck adornment. The man didn't speak as he sat for a moment staring into nothing. He retrieved a deck of cards from the bag he carried and placed the stack in the center of our table. The air around us charged, tinges of electricity pecking at the exposed flesh of my arms and shoulders.

As if the two completed a silent conversation, Clyde reached for the deck then cut it five times. The card placement mimicked a pentacle. The man tapped three times in the empty space in the center before Clyde drew one card from each stack. While he chose the top card from the point stack, he fanned the others out, picking cards at random until the five selected cards sat in the center. The man gathered the remaining cards, returning them to the bag.

A hush descended upon us and for the first time since the man entered the place appeared empty. The tables to our sides were now vacant. Not a sound came from the kitchen. No clanking of plates or running of water. The unnatural silence bothered me though I couldn't understand why. That is until the man flipped over the first card.

Wetness covered me. I was on my back, rocking as water covered my limbs. I'd drowned before, my death beneath the water ushering me into Nero's world eventually leading to my becoming his concubine. But this was different. Instead of only blackness, a light shined at the end of the tunnel. Then we stood before an archway, a giant gate in the center of the city. A figure moved by so fast my mind barely registered it before my insides burned and I dropped to my knees.

I was back in the restaurant then, the cheers from the bar patrons assaulting my ears. Clyde and I were alone. He handed me a drink, insisting I down it in one gulp as he placed a hundred-dollar bill on the table. The liquid burned, keeping my questions at bay before the need to race out of the door took hold. I didn't know where I was going, or why, other than that primal instinct of a Wraith to move. When I hit the sidewalk, I understood. It wasn't the Wraith in me calling. It was the Reaper.

A short-lived scream sent me in the direction of Oakland Cemetery, the stone wall meaning nothing as my scythe materialized. My left hand burned, the parchment appearing with the calligraphy searing its way across the sliver of paper. Two gunshots rang out. The man holding the body of the deceased woman dropped where he stood. I ignored his pleas through the gurgling between his breaths as I approached. The others couldn't see me. I'd slipped into the shadow form that allowed us to collect souls in the open if - and when - the time came.

The woman's essence floated from her body. She stared down at her crumpled flesh draped over the grave of another. I held out the parchment, placing it gently at the glowing feet of the spirit.

"You must choose."

Sad eyes fell on me. "But I'm not ready to go."

"Then know the choice comes but once. If you stay, you can never leave."

She considered my words as the burning ends of the parchment curled over. The blue light followed, the center growing white while the edges stayed blue. The scene on the other side varied from person to person. Sometimes loved ones waited. Or a favorite pet. I often wondered if what they saw was truth or enough illusion to convince them to cross over, only to be thrust into their true fate.

"Quickly now," I encouraged, "you don't have much time."

"But my daughter?"

"Will remember you always."

I was glad my words offered enough comfort that she chose to cross to the other side. But the relief was short lived when rage consumed me. My attention landed on the man whose spirit still clung to the flesh. I waited for the parchment to appear. How dare he survive after taking the life of another? I allowed the anger to nourish me as my scythe burned brighter.

First responders surrounded the man. Medical personnel arrived on the scene, beginning CPR. Clyde stood next to me, our eyes watching the futile attempt to salvage this piece of crap. I watched Clyde's fingers twitch, the tinge of The List calling whether he liked it or not. When the parchment fully formed, I snatched it from his hand then tossed it into the light in the center of the dying man's chest. He could still choose to ignore the portal, but the satisfaction of his demise was enough to bring a smile to my face.

The paramedics moved back, their gloves stripped from their hands as they decided there was nothing left to do to save this man's soul.

"Choose!" I demanded of the confused spirit. He stumbled back, startled. "Go or stay. Choose."

A murder of crows took flight at that moment, the booming of my voice echoing through the masking of power. Animals were more sensitive that way. The man glanced at the two lifeless bodies, and for a moment remorse crossed his face. Then he too stepped through the portal to meet his fate.

* * *

Clyde let me sleep in. And by sleep in I mean he allowed me as much time as I needed before climbing from the bed. I knew he'd want to talk, and not just about our little rogue Reaper problem. He'd never seen me like that before, teetering on the edge of sanity.

I preferred clean collects: nursing homes and old folks. I didn't mind helping the sick rid themselves of their ailments by moving on. He hadn't been there when I'd collected the soul of the one who'd murdered the previous occupant of my current body – though it was my body, to begin with, and she was just keeping it warm for me. I was more than sure Clyde didn't know I was capable of a revenge collect. I knew this would change our dynamic, that he'd from now on question my motives when The List summoned me to return one to the Sands of Time.

I climbed from the bed in my "Hot Stuff" t-shirt and shorts to face the inevitable. Clyde was on the couch, his feet propped up on one of the arms rests as images from the news flashed across the screen. The anchor said something about a woman being murdered in a local cemetery, her attacker falling victim to a gunshot through the chest. The police still hadn't found any suspects and no motive or connection to the pair though it did appear the woman was killed my means other than a gunshot.

"Think they'll find the guy's killer?" I asked as I plopped down in one of the chairs next to the couch.

"Do you really care?"

I didn't know what to say to that. I'm sure he already knew the truth. I also didn't know why he appeared to be annoyed, so I did what he did best, change the subject.

"I'm starving. What's for breakfast?"

"It should be here soon enough." He changed the channel to another news station. The anchor, a brown-haired woman with too much make-up, started with a breaking news story. "We have bigger problems."

We listened in silence as the station flipped to a reporter live on the scene of a mysterious death. Not much information was being released other than the police weren't sure whether to suspect foul play or not. Apparently, they were in the initial stages of the investigation trying to determine who the victim was, how they died, and even if they died where the body was found or placed there later.

"Is this?"

"Yes. Looks like our rogue struck again."

I leaned closer to the television, scanning the reporter's surroundings. "How can you be sure?"

He tapped his shirt pocket. "The Book."

"Oh." Well, that made sense. The Book belonged to the one I was bound too, Death, though we called him Nero. Clyde was the keeper of Nero's tome. The Book of Death, sometimes referred to as The Book of the Dead, told Nero's story, and ours. It didn't always reveal everything about a situation, but when Reapers broke 'the rules,' The Book called to us.

"Lavenia?"

Caught up in thought about then news story, another's stolen time, and The Book, I'd half-forgotten Clyde was there. I didn't like the way he was looking at me. I'd seen that look before, his pretend-to-be innocent look as he contemplated how to snatch the rug from beneath my feet. He'd done it before, his way of reminding me that my lover was Death and I'd damn well better never forget it. Not that I had. I knew good and well what Nero was capable of. Our bond was beyond complicated considering I'd given my life in return for saving the Universe, and the Gods bound us in return as a reminder to him to keep the balance.

"What did you see?" he finally asked.

Feign innocent. "I don't know what you mean."

"That's bullshit, and you know it. We have a rogue Reaper on the loose who obviously is either trying to be caught or so far gone that he's getting sloppy. We don't have time for you to deny your gift."

"Gift. What gift?" A girl could try, right?

"I know you saw something. During the card reveal."

"Who was that man?" I asked. If he could ask questions, so could I.

"It's not important."

"It is to me." I cracked a half smile. I knew that would push him over the edge. I needed to have just a little fun at someone else's expense. All of this seriousness was going to push me over into the land of the rogues, and while I knew if it came down to it, Nero would have me knocked off just like any other regardless of the cost, it didn't mean I couldn't try to see the lighter side of life.

Dammit, Lavenia!" Clyde jumped up, his hand immediately running through his hair as he swung open a cabinet and retrieved a bottle of vodka.

I needed to watch his drinking. He'd been doing it a lot lately, especially after our youngest female made her first jump into an adult body. One female under his guard who could hold her own was one thing. A fledgling female with all of the complexities of being female topped with untested and untrained Wraith capabilities was another.

The guys jumped from one body to another all the time. We were spirits who acted like parasites. Though the bodies we chose were those of the recently departed, we'd discovered that female spirits found it harder to remain long term in a host which meant chasing our spirits around the globe at the drop of a dime. Stability came with age and maturity, but I knew Clyde feared going back to those days when he never knew when his charge would be there or gone. I did have other protectors, but he was big-brother in the house and would always feel responsible for all of us.

"What gave me away?"

He downed the drink before patting the pocket of his button-down shirt.

"Ah. The Book. I should know better by now. Always telling my business. Well, you're right. I did see something. I was in water or floating over it. And I was on my back. There was a tunnel and an arch."

"That makes sense. One of the cards referenced an underground passageway accessible by river. I think it is the Etowah tunnel. And the arch is probably the Millennium Gate."

I considered telling him about the last part, but he had enough on his mind. If he wanted us to go to this Millennium Gate I'd bring it up then.

"What about the others? Weren't there five cards."

"Yes," Clyde answered. "I've already gotten what was needed from the first. The clue was easy, 'find the place where the wall lives and knock three times at the door.'"

"What?"

"The Krog Tunnel. It's not too far from here, so I decided to check it out while you slept. The tunnel walls are a living mural, an artist's dream, graffiti or not. There is a tiny door there which spoke of a place where the eyes stare back at you."

This was getting complicated. "So? What? We are on some sort of scavenger hunt?"

"Seems that way. Though I am wondering…"

His voice trailed off.

"Don't get quiet on me Clyde. What's going through that head of yours?"

A knock on the door gave him a short reprieve. Our food had arrived. I allowed him to spread out breakfast before I started with the grilling. We picked through the offerings: bagels and spreads, fruit, cheese. Even scrambled eggs and waffles.

Plate packed high, mouth stuffed with eggs I did the most unladylike thing when I cornered him. Talk with my mouth full.

"Now spill it."

"Well, as I said, the first card was the reference to the tiny door at the living tunnel. The next was a child's doll head. I suppose that is what the clue from the door refers to as well. I did a little research and discovered a place called Doll's Head trail."

"Is that where we're headed today?"

"Headed?" He raised an eyebrow at my choice of words. "Pun intended?"

"Funny."

He stole a bagel from the bunch, slathering it with strawberry compote. "Your words, not mine."

"Any who. What about the other cards?"

"You know about the river one. And the Millennium Gate."

Clyde must have thought I wasn't keeping track. He explained four out of the five. Or at least he gave me enough to shut me up for specific details. So why avoid the last card.

"And the last one?"

He scooted from the table, retrieving the vodka. He poured a shot for me and a half of a glass full for himself before reclaiming his seat.

"Uh. A little early to be drinking don't you think?"

He held the glass up, examining the contents before commenting, "I think you know how the saying goes. It's five o'clock somewhere."

I stopped him before the glass reached his mouth. "Clyde. What was the last card?"

His glass clanked on the table top before he focused his attention solely on me.

"I am not sure I know the answer. The last card wasn't just one card. The image, it moved. One minute it was black. Then there was a scythe. Then something flashed, and the black came back."

"What do you think it means?"

"I don't want to think about it. Look, get dressed. We need to check out the trail. We're also going to meet a couple of kayakers at the tunnel. Based on the card and your vision I think there is something we either need to know about this Reaper or..."

Normally I would press, but at this juncture, I already had my own shit to deal with, so I left it. We finished breakfast in silence, the news still playing in the background. When we finished, we gathered our things and hit the road.

* * *

"Okay, this is freaky."

I didn't know what to expect from this trip to the park, especially when we turned down a gravel road. Have these people not heard of pavement? The beauty surprised me, the undisturbed nature surrounding the parking at the sign marking the beginning of the trails. We followed the initial path over the boardwalk. While a few families enjoyed the scenery, pointing out to the youngsters the turtles sunbathing in the shallow part of the water and on the logs scattered about, for the most part the place felt isolated. A good place to dump a body during the winter months when few people dared to spend an extensive amount of time exposed to the elements.

Clyde pushed me to use my intuition, something I'd avoided since my falling out with my bedmate. When I tapped into that part of me, the part that bound me to him, he could sense things. Things I kept hidden, things that were mine and mine alone. Not that I think Nero spends his time concerned with the deep dark things I keep tucked into my subconscious. He is Death after all, and he does have souls of his own to collect.

I followed the pull, my attention drawn to one particular doll. At least this one wasn't just a head. While not part of the original design, someone added a third eye adornment using a good ole ball point pen. I stared into the mildewed eyes of the doll and the world faded away. I felt my body falling forward only to discover I was on my back again, staring up at the canopy of trees. I expected to see Clyde there, hovering over me, searching to determine my ailment. But I was alone. Except, I wasn't.

I tried to summon my scythe; my mind focused on the feel of it materializing in my hand only to find nothing there. What the hell was going on? The world shifted, the sun hiding behind darkening clouds when something in the distance drew my attention. I rolled over on all fours staying low to the ground, doing my best to hide in the bushes. As I crawled forward, a green glow cut off my path. Relief washed over me. Green was Clyde's color. I turned, prepared to pull him down to not be seen when my eyes locked on a stranger. I froze, my mind unable to wrap around the image.

Before I comprehended the sight, the figure raised a blade, and I prepared to have my head chopped off, my sprit thrown back into the Void, or worse, condemned to the Sands of Time. But the contact never came. When I opened my eyes, I realized the blade passed right through me. To my right, a head dropped to the ground, empty eyes staring up at me as it lulled over from one side to another.

As I felt the bile rising in my stomach an arm wrapped around my midsection, holding me up. Breakfast spilled from my lips as my insides fought against the churning caused by the vision. I struggled for control as the whisper of my name rang in my ears. Initially, I believe it to be Clyde trying to make sure I was ok. Then it grew louder and stronger and when the word 'run' followed I grabbed Clyde by the wrist, dragging him from the spot where we stood. He didn't ask any questions, just picked up the pace, and eventually tossed me over his shoulder when I slowed us down. We jumped into our rented SUV, the tires digging into the dirt and gravel as we sped away.

"That's two," I said as we continued down the highway. Clyde didn't respond, nor did he slow down until we reached the I-75 interchange and headed north. Eventually, when the road turned to a straight sparsely populated highway, I forced his hand.

"Clyde." I tried to be gentle, playing the girl card. "Please tell me you know what is going on."

His grip on the steering wheel tightened. An indication he either wanted to tell me but wasn't sure how I'd take the news or he really didn't have a clue what was going on. At this point, I'd accept either answer.

"What did you see in your last vision?"

Again, he turned the tables on me. No reason to deny that I'd had another vision. "The green light. A scythe light. I thought it was you." When he chose not to acknowledge the observation, I continued. "In the park, I saw a Reaper with a glowing green scythe cut the head off a man."

"Are you sure it was a man?"

"It was a human head. The eyes stared back at me when it hit the ground," I replied, not sure why he questioned what I saw unless, as usual, he knew more than he was telling.

"I see."

We rode in silence, me wanting to know what he knew. But pushing Clyde only meant more waiting. We'd been down this road so many times it became our norm. He'd give me a little. I'd try to take too much. He'd shut down which left me with little to nothing. This time I decided to ride it out, though it ate me up inside.

He eventually broke the silence. "What makes you think the wielder of the scythe wasn't me?"

Hmm. Hadn't thought much about it. The Clyde who sat in the driver's seat was the only Clyde I'd known.

Don't know whether he and Nero worked out a deal or anything but even when he disappeared for months at a time; he always returned looking like, well, Clyde.

"Another body," I said the words, though I meant them more for myself.

"Yes, Lavenia. Another body. I know who our rogue is. Or at the very least, who's bloodline he belongs to."

I shouldn't have been surprised. But I was. Clyde didn't talk much about his time in other bodies. Not that our other misfits, Billy or Jesse, did either. We jump. It's what we do. One of the many gifts bestowed upon us when we accepted, willingly or not, Nero's sand. The ability to inhabit the bodies of others.

"So, who is he?" I asked.

"She."

Now that surprised me. "She? Since when is there another female Reaper?"

"There were many at one time. Or at least many in the Balance bloodline. Maybe he received the bit of feminine power from Nero. Let psychology tell it every man has just a bit of the feminine in them. DNA and all."

I stopped myself from commenting further. I had to start thinking like a Reaper and not like a Wraith. We were harder; we carried both sides, the ability to collect human souls and Reaper souls. Reapers only held human responsibilities which made them less complex, however slight the difference. The Oracle had tried to explain it all once. 95% of it went over my head so I smiled and nodded and when he was done went about my merry way.

"I suppose I should tell you that I've been hearing the whispers again."

I jerked forward as he slammed on breaks veering off onto the shoulder. Maybe I should have been more tactful with the approach. He threw the vehicle in park before nearly climbing between the seats to look me in the eye.

"Since when?"

He seemed surprised, which told me The Book hadn't warned him of this part of the adventure.

"Since we came through the veil. But only before danger."

Fury burned beneath his cool exterior. I saw it in his eyes. "Why didn't you say anything before?"

"Didn't think it was important. We had other priorities. They were warnings to me. You told me to use my intuition, and I did. The whispers have always come with it."

He gave me the once over, a bit of fear seeping to the surface before he reclaimed the driver's seat. He turned the radio on full blast, silencing any potential conversation until we reached our destination. My skin started to prickle when we hit Dawsonville, the anticipation growing with each stop. By the time we hit Castleberry Bridge Road, every hair on my body stood at attention.

The radio volume dropped when he eased off the gas. Another one of those technology things I didn't understand though the purpose of this one made sense to me.

"I don't like this Clyde," I finally said when he pulled next to a pickup truck. The man and woman were unloading a canoe and kayak as we rolled to a stop.

"You don't have to do this."

"You know I'm the only one who can. Isn't that why you brought me along?" I'm no fool.

Clyde could have brought Billy or Jesse or even Rasul. He chose me for a reason though he would deny it to the end.

"Just know, there is something not right about this whole thing."

"Don't you think I know that?"

Clyde rarely lost his temper. He was Mr. Cool-Calm-and-Collected, the voice of reason between the lust-filled High Priestess, her overbearing Prince, the blond-haired pervert, and Mr. Gather-my-intel-report-back-and-leave-me-alone. I needed him to play his role because right now the High Priestess was about to shit all over her throne.

The driver's door flew open, and Clyde exited without another word. The façade came back immediately, the smile pasted across his face as he greeted the pair. I sank into my seat, my mind racing as I called to the Universe for protection. I walked with Death. He was my bedmate, my concubine, and more than that he was the one I was bound to when I chose to sacrifice myself to save all of life. Though we were currently on the outs, should I need him I knew he'd be there, swooping down like a hawk to pluck me from fate's nasty demise.

Peace. The unexpected whisper of that one word calmed my fears. I ignored the nagging in the back of my mind urging me to call for the speaker. I accepted the stillness washing over me, a renewed sense of being taking up residence until my door opened and Clyde stood before me.

"They're ready whenever you are."

We took the path down to the ‘put in' location according to our guide. The men carried the equipment while we women folk trailed behind.

"First time out?" Teri, the woman by my side, asked as the path started to slope downward.

"Yep. My friend's a little on the adventurous side. He suckered me into coming."

"Oh, this is an adventure. But it's not bad. The water level is perfect today. A nice cruise through the rapids."

Cruise through the rapids huh. I hope her words rang true. We chit-chatted the rest of the way. She filled me in on some basics. Keeping my head low since we were going to be in the canoe and being prepared for the slight drop about a third of the way through. We safety-ed up and climbed into the canoe while Teri's friend Sam took the kayak. Clyde sat in the middle of the canoe, taking on paddling responsibilities. Teri sat in front with me in the back. She instructed me to lie on my back when we entered the tunnel and pay attention.

The water picked up speed as we entered. As suspected, when I hit the darkness my intuition opened. Hieroglyphs played across the top of the cave, my body swaying with the rapids as images of Reapers battled across the stone. There was one, a massive Amazonian figure, who cut down all who crossed her path. The dip interrupted the character play, and as we settled into the faster rapids, another image appeared. One with massive wings and a familiar scythe. They fought hand to hand first, then scythe to scythe until an hourglass appeared between them. The light around the images grew, the outlines becoming fainter until the essence of the woman danced towards the hourglass. A tug of war ensued, the pull between life and death strong in this one until the scythe came down severing the head of the body and the connection to it. We hit light then, the end of the tunnel washing away the last remnants of the collected soul and the one responsible for it.

Clyde only nodded his confirmations as I explained my vision on our return trip. For the first time ever, he gave me the side eye when I requested Varsity for our dinner on the go. Every girl needs a little grease in her life, and nothing compares to real onion rings. He can hate all he wants; I don't give a rat's ass.

Eventually, we hunkered down in the hotel brainstorming our visit to the Millennium Gate Museum. Regardless of the planning and plotting much of our morning activities hinged on walking into the museum and answering the draw to the next location. This was the last one the cards spoke of, and I wasn't sure what to expect.

I welcomed sleep, regardless of the level of fitfulness. My limbs itched for action, my mind playing defense moves over and over until eventually exhaustion grabbed a hold and dragged me into the Sandman's land. The three hours passed by like a whirlwind leaving me lethargic. Clyde shoved a cup of coffee from Community Grounds in my face and stood by as I guzzled the sugar filled brew. Two hours later, we walked into the museum prepared to face our rogue.

Under everyday circumstances I would have taken in the scenery, the beauty of the expanse of culture and history presented. Today was not that day. The moment I stepped foot into the place a pull dragged me to the 18th Century Georgia Pioneer Gallery. Caught in a hypnotic dance with an unknown power, I made it two steps into the entryway before my stomach burned. The pain hadn't hit me yet, but the minute I laid eyes on the blood seeping from my mid-section all sense of reason shot from my body. I doubled over, falling forward; nearly face first had my knees not buckled in the process. The blood continued to spew from the wound, and I went down hard on my right side.

A moment later, the room flashed green. I knew Clyde had my back. He'd neutralize the threat, ensuring both of our safety before letting his guard down enough to check on me. Red bottom shoes stopped in front of me. Clyde was right, this one was female, and at the moment I was helpless. I hate being helpless.

She didn't live long. She must have thought I was alone. I blinked. A thud followed, and there on the ground, bathed in a green glow lay a severed head. The wide eyes searched my soul, for what I did not know. I wanted to convince myself that the blonde staring back at me was the head of a mannequin tipped over by a passerby. But I knew better. Though the face was different, the vision before confirmed that this Reaper could only be collected by severing the head. The body dropped before darkness consumed me and all was at peace.

* * *

I wished it was the beeping of machines that drew me from my slumber. Half awake, memories of the short time in the museum coaxed me into the presence. That and the impending rage storming closer. To open my eyes or not? I pondered as heat beat away the cold sterility of my surroundings. A little surprised, the stale emptiness of the room confirmed I was in a hospital, though with our gifts that realization came with a shit load of confusion.

"Sir! Sir! You can't go in there."

I assumed the nurse was attempting to stop the lone figure barreling closer to my room. I felt not only his rage, but the underlying worry fueling it. Then it all went quiet. When I finally opened my eyes, Clyde leaned forward.

"I tried my best to keep your condition a secret," he said before the door swung open, "but I can only keep so much from them."

My eyes locked with the ebony warrior, my Prince of the Nai, standing in the doorway. His imposing stature made the room suddenly smaller. The scars on his arms shimmered with silver, a testament to his years of battle and the painstaking process the Nai used to heal their wounds.

My Priestess. Rasul's words were spoken only in my head.

"My Prince." I knew he'd come for me. I was the High Priestess of the Nai, and he was the King of the Prince of Nai, those born to serve and protect the priestesses at all cost. Unlike the others, who were born for their priestesses, Rasul was said to be born 'of' his. We still did not understand the difference, though Clyde hinted that The Book held the secret and would reveal it when the time was right.

He crossed the room, his hand coming to rest on mine as Clyde vacated the seat next to the bed. No words needed to be spoken. I knew why he was here and what I needed to do. His head came to rest on my chest, his eyes fluttering closed as he silently requested I do what was required. And I did. I took from him, fed from his energy until I'd had my fill. The last thing I remembered was him scooping me from the bed. He'd take me home. To the place, I needed to be our new home away from home.

Another Day in the A

By

Violette L. Meier

I used to hate my life. Everything was so freaking blah until I met him. He changed my perspective on it all. Now I live everyday like it is my last. I know you women are rolling your eyes saying to yourself, "Why she gotta get saved by a man? Save yourself!" This is not that kind of story so relax. I guess it is better to say that he helped me change my perspective. Because of him, I've learned to love hard and live free! Carpe Diem is my motto and I am happier for it. Why am I so ecstatic you ask? Allow me to explain.

I am not new to Atlanta. I was born here. Living in Atlanta and being from Atlanta is like being a unicorn. Native Atlantans are indeed a rare breed. I grew up on Patterson Avenue near where Memorial Drive crosses Moreland Avenue in East Atlanta; not too far from

Kirkwood or Little Five Points. My neighborhood was old and full of great old people. Everyone knew everyone and everyone looked out for everyone. My Uncle Cyrus walked me home from school every day before he went back up the street to sit on the wall across from the liquor store and drank himself unconscious. Once I found him lying in Mr. Moore's yard, and I ran home screaming because I thought death had taken him. Fortunately, it was just Colt 45. My grandfather and my Uncle Willie had to carry him home as I walked behind them in a trail of tears.

By the time I was in middle school, I walked myself to school and I became immune to my uncle's harmless drunkenness, the root worker and her gang of hounds, people arguing with street poles, and overage boys who waved for me to follow them into their homes with candy in one hand and the other hand on their crotches. I learned to ignore, and ignore I did. Living in the city of Atlanta one had to learn to ignore many things.

By high school I moved to DeKalb County where I discovered it was greater in Decatur. I was popular in high school and realized that I was piping hot. At first, I was not aware of this. I was very unconscious of my physical. I was more interested in fashion and poetry. I was made aware that I was fine by mean upper-class girls and nice upper-class boys. I never did rediscover the meaning of humility. There was no need. If you got it, flaunt it, and I did.

Soon, it was back to Atlanta for college. I got my education in the middle of the AUC. There is no greater education for a black person than one from an HBCU. College was full of exploration, lust, and learning. FreakNik stole my innocence and someone stole my identity when I lost my purse during registration. I partied myself onto academic probation but redeemed myself until I graduated Cum Laude. Honesty, it was thankya Lordie, but the first sounds better. When I finally graduated, I moved into a one-bedroom apartment off Peachtree Street near the Fox Theater. There, I hobbled in and out of my apartment everyday like a lifeless zombie. I worked, ate, slept, and did it all over again day after day. I worked as a program director for a nonprofit organization that I did not believe in nor did they seem to believe in me. I hated my life. I hated my life because I had no life. I had no man, no fun, no real friends, nothing! My life sucked and frankly I was tired of living it. Every day was a mindless hustle to support a life I wasn't fully living. I couldn't remember the last time I painted, wrote a poem, or danced. I didn't do anything I loved doing anymore and I couldn't understand what was stopping me. I guess I became used to complaining and misery became comfortable.

When the first hot summer day came that year, I had decided to accept an invite to a swanky "all white" pool party. I squeezed my big bootie in the slinkiest white bikini I could find, pulled my gigantic afro into a puff ball, put on some diamond hoop earrings, four-inch heels, grabbed my bag and made my way to the party. My life sucked, but at least I was cute. The mirror was always kind, the only thing that was ever kind.

The house was generous and right smack in the middle of Buckhead! I pulled through the gated driveway and watched as the gate closed slowly behind me. Trees covered the house from the street, hiding the mammoth mansion from outside viewers. A valet took my car, and I made my way through the house to the pool out back.

Glistening black bodies dipped in and out of the water as laughter floated through the air. I sat on a pool chair posing like I had a personal photographer. My friend Princess (she gave herself that name by the way- her real name was Noreeva) sat next to me chattering nonstop about some weird bearded dude sitting across from us staring at me like a piece of steak. He was hot but something about him was unnerving so I rolled my eyes, tuned her out, and laid back to let the hot sun turn my yellow skin brown.

The lower the sun got, the stronger the smell of weed became and the more cups ran over with cocktails. I drank, flirted, and drank some more. Noreeva had long left me for a new boy toy. See, that's what I'm talking about. No real friends! I was kinda jealous. I hadn't been touched by a man in so long that I was sure that my hymen had regenerated. Not that men didn't try to holla; it's just that there was always something wrong with them like the last guy who walked over to introduce himself. He was very handsome but one of his ears was noticeably smaller than the other. I cut the conversation short. Noreeva told me I was being extra. I rolled my eyes and took another sip. It didn't matter. The party sucked like everything else had sucked lately so I decided to go home. I stood up, one butt cheek completely out of my bikini bottom, my ankles twisting in my heels because I was way too tipsy for balance, but I made my way to the valet anyway. An odd looking pink man hesitantly handed me my car keys after I yelled at him twice to hand them over. He shook his head and walked away after he saw me swerve down the driveway.

I turned down Peachtree and drove towards home, my car struggling to stay in its lane. I prayed that the APD was somewhere harassing some "up and coming" rapper. Lord knows there was one of them on every block. I passed Amtrak, SCAD, The High Museum, and soon the sign for The Fox came into view. I was home. My car pulled into my lot as I fumbled to find my parking pass. I let myself in after dropping the pass several times on the car floor. At an angle, my car swerved into two parking spaces and stopped. I opened my door and spilled out like the two cocktails I drank. Oh, I forgot to mention that I am not a drinker. A matter of fact, I had never drunk anything before that night. I mean nothing. Not a thing! I figured my life wasn't happy sober so I might as well try it drunk.

Every eye was on me as I shuffled down the hallway with my bikini wedgie, which looked like a thong by now, hardly putting one foot in front of the other. I somehow made the wrong turn and walked into the workout room. It was empty, dark, and surprisingly unlocked considering it was supposed to be closed at 11:30pm and it was 3:12 in the morning. I stumbled forward and lost my footing. My butt hit the floor hard. I was too drunk to cry. I grabbed hold to the end of a barbell and tried to pull myself up but my ankle twisted and the side of my head slammed into the end of the barbell. Everything went black.

When I woke up, I was sober and there *he* was. He was sitting on the bench next to the barbell that had laid me out. Tall, dark, slender but muscular with a shiny beard and mysterious eyes; kinda sexy. He could get it. I looked down at his feet and there I was lying in a pool of scarlet liquid. I blinked and looked again. I was confused. How could I be standing and looking eye to eye with him and be on the floor?

"Velvet," he said. "Finally, nice to meet you." He pulled a fat cigar from his pocket and crossed his legs. He was dressed in a polo style shirt, a crisp pair of jeans, and a wristwatch that seemed to sparkle with an eerie sheen.

"Who are you?" I asked. I wouldn't say I was scared but seeing my body at his feet was a bit disconcerting.

"You know me," he answered taking a puff; his watch glowing in the smoke like a lighthouse in the night.

"No, I don't!" I snapped, but something in me knew who he was. My soul recognized him.

"You ready?" he asked.

"Ready for what?" I stammered nervously as I locked and unlocked my fingers. My eyes darted between his eyes and my body. He sat there quietly smoking, waiting for me to make up my mind.

"You know what," he answered looking at his watch. "Time is precious. Make up your mind."

I looked into his eyes, then back at my body. My stomach thundered. If a spirit or whatever the heck I was could sweat, that is what I was doing, and I was doing it hard.

"Life sucks. Right?" he said between puffs, his brown eyes piercing and captivating.

I looked down at my body and went into a mental panic. For some reason, it wasn't until his words that I realized that I was actually dead. Seeing my body didn't even drive home that fact. It was his question. His eyes. His watch that made me realize that I was out of time.

"No!" I squealed. "I love my life!" Tears streamed down my face. My feet moved from side to side as I squeezed my hands together. Thoughts of my parents, siblings, and friends flooded my mind. Memories of girl trips, graduations, first love, college sweethearts, and job promotions danced around in my head. Hopes of getting married, seeing the world, having children, growing old bubbled up in my chest.

"I have a family who loves me and a good job. I have my own apartment and a little money in the bank," I blubbered, snot running into my mouth.

"Interesting," he said, a slight smile on his face. "You said your life sucked."

"I know I can be a little ungrateful, and disinterested, and bored, and dissatisfied with everything, but I love my life! I do. I really do!" I cried seeing my body cold and unmoving near the tip of his expensive sneakers. Every time he looked at his watch I felt like all hope was gone. "I have so many things to do and places to go. I still have 325 things to cross off my bucket list."

He stood up and I thought I would crap myself. He moved towards me. I wanted to step backwards but could not move my legs. I wasn't even sure that I still had legs. Maybe the bottom half of my body was a whiff of smoke or something. I looked down and there they were. I breathed a sigh of relief, but that was short lived when I found myself almost nose to nose with this strange man.

"Now you wanna live?" he asked almost rhetorically, as if he was scoffing at my back peddling.

"Yes," I whimpered.

"How bad you want it?" he smirked a smirk that made my stomach flip in a way that I could not decide if it was good or bad.

"Real bad," I whispered.

He stepped closer and grabbed the back of my head. I thought I would die; again. His lips touched mine. He parted my mouth with his tongue and kissed me so deeply and completely I almost considered staying dead if this is what heaven felt like. His lips were soft, but his kiss firm. I felt it all over my body. The kiss lasted what felt like seven days and seven nights.

"Then live," he whispered into my mouth, his dark hands holding the sides of my face.

I swallowed his breath like spun sugar. He pulled back and was gone; faded into the air like his cigar smoke. Only the smell of his cologne lingered. I was on the floor. I sat up holding my bloody head. I looked around the empty, dark workout room. There was no one there but me. After I managed to take my shoes off, I pulled myself to my feet and stumbled into the hallway. Using the wall as a support, I made my way to the reception desk and fainted. When my eyes opened again, I was staring up into the green eyes of a nurse. I looked down at my wrist at a band that read "Grady Memorial Hospital" along with my name: Velvet Covingtree. I shook my head. I knew I was going to be there all night.

"Hey there. Are you okay?" she asked, cleaning my wound.

I nodded; my eyes trying to focus on her face which was stern but kind.

"You have quite a cut, but the wound has been stitched and the scarring should be minimal. What happened?" she asked while writing on a clip board.

"Another day in the A," I responded with a crooked smile. "You wouldn't believe me if I told you."

Blerd and Confused

By

Alan D Jones

Saturday night and the streets of Atlanta were hot and ready to pop off. Word on the street was that a city of Atlanta employee had sold the addresses and Social Security numbers of every Atlanta resident to some offshore third party, who'd saddled everyone with $200,000 of fraudulent debt. This shutdown credit for anyone with a metro address. That in turn caused a run on the banks, leaving most of the locals with only lint in their pockets. But I'd heard whispers from the underground that our sorrow had just begun.

From my high-rise balcony, as I pondered what might be next, a voice from the darkness called out to me.

"Hey, you gonna drink that?"

Of course, the owner of that voice downed my drink before I had a chance to reply. I gave dude a look and he spouted, "Oh, my bad."

It was my neighbor, Grimes, named so because he's, well, grimy. He's in his studio apartment all day, doing only God knows what, except bathing. Add to that his taste for other people's leftovers (interpret that in any way you see fit), and he got pegged as "Grimes". And yet, we deemed Grimes, Lord of the Underworld, because of his fluency in any and all things which exist off the grid.

Grimes tells everyone that he supports himself by buying and selling things on eBay all day. But I know that's a lie. Some time ago while investigating a matter, I came upon the fact that he hosts a website where he performs certain acts upon himself for money. Naturally, he gets paid in Bitcoin. Of course, I've not told the others, and I won't.

Just as I began to turn back towards the city, onto the balcony rolled up my frenemy Marketing Girl.

"Hi, Blerd Boy!"

"That's not my name."

"Well, it should be. It's called alliteration, *Blerd Boy.* It helps people remember you name."

"You do realize that name recognition would make me useless?"

"Whatever." She smiled wryly. Teasing me is her favorite sport.

A third guest joined us on the balcony. It was Oliver (aka Money) Penthouse, owner and options trader (which simply means that he's a walking, breathing, gambling addiction in nice suit). More importantly, he's Marketing Girl's "Mistake", as she often calls him when he's not around.

Money smiled at Marketing Girl. "Hi Jeanene, where's Fluffy?"

"She's in doggie daycare for the weekend, so I'm ready for whatever," she answered and said nothing else, except to give me an *I can't believe I did this*, eye roll. Icy still months later, after hooking up with Money. And while alcohol was involved, to her credit Marketing Girl owned what happened. In a dating sense, Oliver liked to keep his "options" open. Marketing Girl, no prude, was deeply concerned how being another mark on Oliver's bedpost might hurt her brand. However, to his credit, Money had a firm grip on discretion.

Oliver, wealthy but not rich, stepped past Grimes towards me.

"Blerd."

"Money."

I shook his hand and dapped him up. We were totally different cats, but I'd been helping him launch a couple of side hustles. Oliver realized some time ago that his profession was one that would eventually devour its host. And the first step towards salvation is always recognizing that you have a problem. And to be honest, Money's career path was beneath the station into which he was born.

See, in this country, while we sell the dream of social mobility, the reality is that we have caste system which is just as entrenched as any in this world. Money is third generation college educated, Ivy Schooled and his parents (a doctor and an attorney, no less) have a place in the Hamptons he's expected to visit for several weeks each summer, take on a respectable profession and marry someone in his class, whenever he decides to settle down. Again, wealthy, not rich. Marketing Girl is second generation college educated. Daddy was a small business owner, mama a VP for regional bank. Her folks took pride in being able to send her to a private school and being able to pay for more than half of her HBCU college education. She's expected to marry (college degreed only) and produce two to three beautiful grandchildren for Mommy and Daddy to open 529 college saving funds for. In the meantime, she takes trips with her single, college educated, upper middle-class girlfriends to bucket list locations far and wide. So, while she may visit the Hamptons (if someone invites her), she knows she'll never belong. As for me, I (and my cousin) am a first-generation college graduate (Georgia Tech). Born into a single parent household in the projects, the world expected me to be dead or to at least have a prison record by this point in my life. In this regard, I've been a big disappointment. And why would I want to visit Hamptons? Then there's Grimes. Mama was an addict. Spent half his childhood in foster homes. Tests very well. Gets into colleges. Can't finish things. Loses focus. ADD like a mug. There's a warrant with his name on it in Suffolk County.

As Marketing Girl stared into the streets below, she asked, "So, what's the latest?"

I turned back towards everyone. "Well, first I was able to confirm that it wasn't a city employee behind this. Yes, the information came from his work account, but he was hacked by parties unknown."

Marketing Girl injected, "But the city is more than willing to let old boy take the fall, right?"

"Of course. City leadership feels it's better for the people to have someone to blame," I answered, having seen some unsecured emails posted around the net to that effect.

Oliver, following up on the previous day's status report, lifted his mixed drink towards me and asked, "So, have you determined their end game?"

"No, but we think we have a good lead." I nodded towards Grimes.

Grimes eyes opened as though he was just coming out of a trance.

"Yeah, the homeless crew I run with is really spooked, which is odd when you consider none of them has any credit to damage. Anyway, they wouldn't talk about it on the street, so we're supposed to meet them in the shantytown off Jefferson Tonight."

I added quickly, "So, now that we're all here, we need to get going." This little crew of mine formed almost two years ago around a common interest in things which just didn't seem right. Suffice it to say, we're a group of well-intentioned folks who major in resolving left field stuff. The team brings me sideways stuff, I look into it and if it has any merit, we pursue the matter.

Grimes asked, "Aren't you gonna wait for your cousin *Kisha*?" (Note: Kisha is not my cousin's name, but for the sake of this account that's what we'll call her. Why I'm doing this will become apparent later in this tale).

"She's double parked downstairs waiting for us. I figured we'd need two cars."

Well, we get downstairs, and Grimes immediately heads for Kisha's ride, at which point Kisha popped out of the driver's door and to hold up her hand like a huge flashing stop sign.

"No, Grimes. You know good and well, you're not riding in my car. I'm still paying for this ride, and your non-bathing self cannot ride in it. I don't know why you're even trying me. You know the deal."

It was apparent to all that Grimes was smitten with Kisha. Grimes loved hood girls, but most of them would have nothing to do with him.

And mind you, Kisha was a forensic accountant, and was in the process of applying to law schools. But as Kisha herself would tell you, "I'm an educated, refined woman, but my hood-ness is on a hair trigger." With our mothers being as close as they were, the two of us grew up more like siblings, down the street from one another. And yet, somehow the whole code-switching thing never really took with me. But on the real, the ability to flip on a dime is a valuable survival trait in "*dem streets*". But we're even more tightly bound for another reason. Back in the day some dude went sideways on Kisha, and I had to handle it. The events of that day are the one thing we do not speak of.

I called out, "Come on Grimes, you can ride with me. We'll meet you guys there."

Once alone in my car Grimes asks me, "So, what's your cousin got against me?"

I gave Grimes a look, like you "you really want to know?"

He gestured back, arms and palms up, like "come on with it…."

"Well, a couple of things come to mind right off. First, there's the personal hygiene thing…"

Grimes interrupted me, "Well, of course I'd bathe before going out with her."

"Dude, you do realize that in modern society, washing one's self on the regular is kind of expected, like even when you don't have a date?"

"Yeah, I got you. What else?"

"Well, then there's the whole random chic thing."

Grimes chirped in again, "Hey, I'd told y'all a hundred times before, I have an understanding with some of the ladies who need a spot for a night every now and then. They're welcome to spend the night, no strings attached. They get a hot shower and a warm place to lay their heads for a night. If things go down, great; but you know me; I'd never force or even coerce anyone to do anything."

"I know that Grimes, but…"

"If everybody benefits, what's the problem? You know it's really a double standard. Oliver sleeps around on the regular, and everyone's cool with it. But just because *some* of the women I bring over are struggling, it's an issue. It's classism and it's not right."

"Perhaps. But I tell you what, when you invite these women over, why don't you let them have your condo and you come camp out in my spare bedroom? I mean, if you're doing this just because you're a good guy, what should it matter? Are you down with that?"

Grimes gave me a look as he tried to find the words to answer, but his prolonged silence was all the answer I needed.

"Bruh, forget about Kisha. You might want to check yourself before checking for someone else. I'm just saying." Since I've known him, Grimes has always had trouble accepting cultural norms. I'm sure it's some kind of personality disorder or what not, but then again most of the time his insights are valid. But in this case, he's rationalizing and shows to me that perhaps that he really doesn't know his own self yet.

We parked and began our descent to the shantytown. But as Grimes and I neared our goal I began to hear what sounded like whimpering. The two of us edged closer, and as we did I saw Marketing Girl on her knees sobbing uncontrollably. Cousin Kisha was frantically walking back and forth, with her hands covering her ears, as she yelled and screamed into the atmosphere. Oliver stood beneath one of the bodies reciting "Southern trees bear a strange fruit…"

Seeing me, the typically emotionally detached Oliver called, "Come help me get them down."

Grimes stepped past me to Oliver. "Wait. Let's think about why they're here?"

I saw where Grimes was going. "There are easier ways to kill someone, but you lynch someone to send a message."

Grimes added, "Or you want to incite somebody."

"Or some bodies…" Oliver caught on. "So, this needs to stay out of the press, for now anyway."

Marketing Girl, stepped in. "I know the mayor's chief of staff. I'll give her a call."

Grimes stepped past me further into the darkness towards a particular body which caught his eye.

"Shit…, it's Mary. Oh Mary, this was not your crew, why were you here? Blerd, help me get her down, please…"

Oliver started, "But the police…"

I raised my hand to him before turning to help Grimes. I climbed up into tree to untie the knot holding Mary aloft, lowering her into the arms of Grimes, Marketing Girl and Kisha, who'd stopped pacing by this point.

Grimes spoke as he held Mary. "Her face is not disfigured like the others."

"Then she must have been dead before they hung her," I replied as I descended from the tree.

Grimes added, "Yeah, she must have put of a fight. That's my Mary."

I took out my flashlight and began looking for clues. I figured that I had about thirty minutes before the police arrived, given the logistics of notifying them and the coroner through back channels. I paced back and forth looking for answers; I even checked a couple of the nearby shacks for something, anything. Then in the twenty-eighth minute, I looked up again at the victims. I finally realized that the answer was right in front of me. One of the guys wore City of Atlanta Water department overalls, as did the woman.

I came to a full stop to ask Grimes, "Did Mary work at the water plant too?"

"Yes, she'd just started working at the Water Department a few weeks ago. One of the guys here, Joe, hooked her up. She told me that she was hoping to get off the street before the end of the year."

"I think that we need to pay the closest water treatment facility a visit, like right now. Grimes you drive, I need to look something up."

We reached our destination in less than ten minutes and parked across the street in an empty lot. In route to our destination, I was able to hack into the water department's back office system and execute a data crawling routine that captured disruptions in any established data patterns. Having gotten my results, I handed my laptop to Kisha.

"Cuz, take a look."

Kisha was excellent at her job and I knew that if there was any activity in the last thirty days which was funky, she'd find it. In less than ten minutes, she let out an "Hmm…" I knew that tone well.

"I'm seeing that they ordered some chemicals last month that were outside of their normal supply. And I'm betting that the dummies bought this stuff in the proportions they intend to use."

"Cuz, you know it's always around the money where they slip up. Let me see."

Looking at what they ordered and how much of each substance, I was able to determine what our unknown villains were looking to create. It was a variant of fluoroquinolone, a chemical compound known to cause psychosis in humans. We were sure that the variation in their compound was done to make the effects even more acute.

Hearing the facts, Oliver was puzzled.

"I don't get it."

I addressed him, "Yo, Money. Think about it. Freeze up the credit of anyone with a metro Atlanta address, cause a run on the banks, push out a psychosis causing chemical into the water system in a largely African-

American city, and then light the match. Lynch a bunch of brothers right in the middle of town. Whoever is behind this wants to start a race war."

We all gave a collective groan at the gravity of the situation. Marketing Girl, after releasing an explicative, asked, "So, what do we do now?"

I replied as I grabbed my bag of tricks from the trunk of my car. "Well, Kisha, Grimes and I are going over there to see what's up, while you call 911 and Money calls Homeland Security." Oliver, didn't have them on speed dial or anything, but he knew people. When we need access, Money is who we call.

Kisha and Grimes flanked me as we made our way across the street. I used my bolt cutters to gain access to the treatment plant. My thought was to see if these fools were actually doing this, and to stop them if they were. A simple goal, right?

We walked right up to the security desk, and I addressed the woman staffing that post. She asked right off, "Who are you and how did you get in here?"

I answered her, "We're friends of Mary and Joe, and they had some concerns about some new folks hanging around here today."

The security guard tilted her head slightly. "Well, the feds did send in a new testing crew this evening, who said that our PH level were out of balance. But then oddly, they said that they had a tanker truck sitting right outside the gates that was full something that would set things right. They're over there setting up now. But you can't go over there. You're not authorized."

I replied, "And if we do?"

"I'll have to call the police."

"Then please do, and with a quickness."

As the security guard called for backup, we stepped over to where the workers were setting up. I noticed that all of the crew was around the back of the tanker still assembling the tubing. I motioned towards Kisha and she knew what I wanted. She strolled around back and hollered, "Hey guys, anybody got a cell phone I can borrow? My car's broken down and I need to make a call." Those guys couldn't move fast enough to assist her.

In the meantime, Grimes popped the hood of the tanker, and I crawled into the engine. In less than twenty seconds, I disabled the engine, which in turn made the pump on the back end inoperative. Hearing the engine cutoff, those guys all hustled around to the front of the truck. Seeing Grimes in the cab one of them called out, "What the hell…?"

The gang of them began grabbing at Grimes legs trying to pull him down and out. Kisha ran around as I jumped down to Grimes' defense.

"Hey, let him go!" Kisha and I tussled with the men trying to pull them off of Grimes. I hollered at them, "It's a done deal; the police are on their way!"

Stunned, the apparent foreman asked, "You called the police?"

As Money and Marketing Girl ran in with the security guard, and approaching police sirens grew louder, the foreman bolted. Seeing their leader flee, the seemingly befuddled remaining crew took off too, even though they weren't quite sure why they were running. The security guard ran after them, but we all knew that she wasn't going to catch any of them.

Kisha pulled my arm. "I got a name. When I was online, I got the guy's name."

I replied, "And I bet whoever it is, doesn't plan to be around when all hell breaks loose in the morning."

We both looked at Money.

"Sure, y'all go do what you do, Jeanene and I will tie up things here."

Marketing Girl, asked, "Please be careful…"

Back at my ride, Grimes took the wheel as Kisha and worked furiously on our laptops in the backseat.

Grimes asked, "So, what's the name?"

Kisha replied, "Marvin Williams."

"Like the basketball player who played for the Hawks?" Grimes asked.

"Yes, but it's not that Marvin Williams," I answered.

"Okay, I got his address. He's in a high-rise at 14th and Peachtree. Damn, just three blocks from my place."

Grimes acknowledged. "Got it. Hold on, cause y'all know we're running all these *mofo* lights."

As we broke every known traffic law in route to our destination Kisha, blurted out, "You do know that Jeanene likes you, right?"

"What? The way she rides me?" I looked Kisha hard.

Grimes chimed in from the front seat. "Yeah, she's right about that."

Kisha continued. "Cuz, you're the smartest guy I know, but you're so clueless sometimes."

"Totally, clueless!" Grimes added, just as he ran up on a curb nearly hitting a guy, to get around a line of cars sitting at a stop light.

Kisha gave the back of Grimes' head a *"are you crazy"* stare so hard that I know he felt it.

"Yes, she likes to tease you, but never in a mean way, more like a little grade school girl who can't keep the name of the little boy who sits next to her everyday out of her mouth."

"When did you come to this conclusion?"

"Soon after we all got together to do these things."

Grimes laughed. "Clueless, just clueless."

As we neared Marvin Williams' address, I asked one last question. "And, Money?"

"And? Are you looking to marry a virgin? Then what does it matter? And trust me; you wouldn't be breaking any sort of Bro code. Money don't care, cause he's darn near a sociopath when it comes to dating. She does get a little shady when she's had a few drinks. I have literally saved her butt a few times. But I think what went down with Money has really changed her for the better."

Kisha was Marketing Girl's designated driver. Kisha also served to block would be suitors when she's had too much to drink. But on that fateful night, Kisha was on date of her very own.

We double parked the car, ran inside and hopped into the elevator with someone going up, and punched our floor as they swiped their security card for their own floor.

Kisha leaned to me. "Look, Tonight has me feeling some kind of way. None of us knows when our time will come, particularly these days. I just don't want you to miss out on what good can come from this life. Jeanene plays the party girl, but on the real, like most girls she just wants someone she can depend on, the whole security thing. Past a certain age, that's pretty much what all women want; only how they define it varies."

"And what about you?"

"If it happens, it happens. But you know we hood girls aren't looking to be rescued, we expect struggle and to do so alone. We are conditioned to see the pursuit of anything else being as fruitful as chasing the morning vapors. It's a hard thing to let go of, but I'm working on it."

Grimes gave us both a look as if to speak, but the bell rang for our floor. We stepped out and quickly found Marvin's door. I started to knock, but Grimes shook his head and pulled out a crowbar (I have no idea where he hid it). He jammed it into the door and with my assistance we pried the door open and burst into the room. A surprised Marvin, sitting on his balcony enjoying a glass of white wine, sprung to his feet. We pushed past the two suitcases sitting in his living room to box him in on the balcony before he could flee or grab anything like a knife or a gun.

But then right before our eyes, Marvin transformed from a man in fear for his life, to an asshole hosting the biggest shit eating grin ever seen. The villain of the hour plopped back down into his chair and lit a fresh cigar. After taking a puff, he exclaimed, "I can only guess that somehow you hacked into our back-office system and found my name in the paperwork. I order chemicals like those all the time. Maybe those guys with the tanker messed up the mix. If you caught them before they poisoned the city, I say great. Congratulations! Since I didn't stand to benefit from any of this, I'm as surprised by all of this as you are." Marvin gave a wink, before taking another sip.

Working through it all in my own head I realized, as I'm sure my teammates did, this cat had sense enough not to get paid via any traceable form (even if his efforts on the front end were as sloppy as can be).

Grimes sighed. "Krypto, he got paid in some sort of blockchain."

Dumbfounded, Kisha asked, "How could you do this to all of your brothers and sisters?"

Marvin stood and leaned against the balcony railing -- glass in one hand, cigar in the other-- said into the night air as his left hand swept out over the city, "The powers that be, proclaimed that this should be. Thus, it was inevitable. So, why would one not to seek to profit from it?

Such a person would be no different from the war profiteers way back when, who became admired and beloved household names."

A very angry, nearly in tears Grimes asked, "And what about the homeless folks strung up in the park?"

"Oh, that. Who knew the homeless guy working at the plant was a chemist before the pipe got him? But in disposing of that problem, it also served as the spark needed to burn this city down once again."

From somewhere inside of me a pronouncement rose up, "The Universe will not let this rest."

Marvin laughed as he turned back towards the city, "Bruh, miss me with that. In this life, the only real thing is that green paper."

"I'm sorry to hear that." Kisha said, as she moved quickly towards Marvin and in one quick, fluid motion she grabbed Marvin by his legs lifting him up and over the balcony railing. Not two seconds later we heard a car alarm screaming down below.

Kisha didn't even bother to glance over the rail, but simply said to me, "Well, I guess that's two." Meaning that we now had a second thing we'd never speak of again. She walked back past Grimes and me offering, "At least he's at peace now."

Grimes turned to follow Kisha as she exited Marvin's place, "Amen, sister."

I shook my head, before following them out. Passing through the doorway, I exhaled, "He was so distraught."

Kisha pushed the down button, "...and confused."

* * *

The scene was the Starbucks at the Marketplace on Ponce. The crew present was Grimes, Marketing Girl and me. Marketing Girl was debriefing me as Grimes sat off to the side signifying (his favorite pastime).

Marketing Girl smiled. "So, bottom line, the City has no interest in pursuing what went on up on that balcony. They're fine with ruling it a suicide, given the foreman's statement and that all the paperwork led back to Marvin." The truth of the matter was that the City, State and Feds wanted this incident to quietly go away.

From the sidelines Grimes offered a "Cool…"

I sighed in relief, "Thanks, Jeanene."

Marketing Girl smiled as she slid a folder over to me, and speaking quickly as she does when she's excited, "No problem. Now on to new business, and we may want to call in Voodoo Priestess for this one. I know, I know, but just listen, outside of Cancun some bodies showed up missing their brains. So, I'm calling this case, *No Brains South of the Border…*"

Grimes nearly spit out the iced green tea he was sipping through his nostrils. He held up a hand to excuse himself, "Sorry y'all." After he stood, but before exiting, Grimes offered, "Y'all don't see it? Never mind, I'll just step outside for a few." I swear that his emotional development halted at fifteen.

After Grimes left but before Marketing Girl could go on, I reached over and touched her hand, "Hold on a sec; while Grimes is gone, I wanted to ask you something. Would you be willing to go out with me?"

Marketing Girl replied, "What do you mean? We go out for lunch two or three times a month, on top of these little meetings and the occasional Happy Hours."

"No, I mean like to dinner, a dinner date. Somewhere nice, just you and me."

Jeanene's eyes watered, as she gripped my hand back, "Yes, I'd love to."

Piggy Back

By

Milton Davis

Ray pressed the 9mm against the target's head but couldn't pull the trigger.

"What you waiting on, man?" Snatch said. "Blow this bastard."

Ray's finger tensed on the trigger. The bastard, Tony Germello, looked at him side-eyed. No fear showed in his gaze. As a matter of fact, he smiled.

"Fuck this!"

Snatch yanked the gun from Ray's hand the fired two rounds into Tony's head. The body collapsed on the hardwood floor, bright blood oozing from the wounds.

Snatch handed the gun back to Ray.

"Come on, let's go," he said.

Snatch strode toward the door of the abandoned house. Ray stood still, staring at Tony's body. This wasn't his first hit, nor would it be the last. But it was something about the way Tony looked at him, as if it wasn't over.

"Man, you coming?"

Ray shoved his hands into his wool jacket then took on a cool demeanor.

"Why you in a hurry? Ain't nobody in this neighborhood gonna call the cops."

"I'm cold, that's why. Let's go."

They crossed the weed choked backyard then climbed the rusted fence into the yard of the abandoned ranch house where the stolen van was parked. Snatch clambered into the driver's seat while Ray trotted around to the passenger side. They took their time, easing into the middle of the street then cruising to the nearest highway entrance.

Snatch turned on the radio then began whistling the familiar song. Ray was quiet, staring at his shaking hands. What the hell was wrong with him? He saw Tony's eyes, those staring, unflinching eyes. He wasn't scared at all, he wasn't even arrogant. It was if he didn't care, as if he had it all planned out.

"Snatch, you believe in God?" Ray said.

Snatch chuckled. "If I did I wouldn't be doing this for a living unless I had a thing about Hell."

Snatch looked him in the eye. "You ain't about to go saved on me, are you?"

"Naw, man. I was just thinking. Tony looked at us as if he knew he had somewhere better to be."

"Tony was crazy," Snatch said. "That's why he got popped. Is that why you wouldn't do him?"

"No." Ray fidgeted in his seat. "Just didn't feel right."

Snatch took the exit to downtown.

"Let me off right here," Ray said.

"I can take you all the way," Snatch replied.

"That's okay. I feel like walking."

Snatch swerved the van into the nearest park. He reached into his coat pocket then pulled out a wad of hundreds. He counted out half then gave them to Ray.

"This is the last time I pay you something for nothing, friend or not," he said. "Don't punk out on me next time."

Ray shoved the money into his coat pocket. "See ya, bruh."

"Yeah."

Ray buttoned his coat as he hopped out the van. He strolled up Peachtree to Kiley's. The bar was near empty, two patrons sitting face to face in a booth near the back in what sounded like a heated argument. Ray glanced at them then sat at the bar. Eileen sauntered up to him, wiping a beer mug.

"Hey Ray. What you having?"

"Dead Hitler."

"Ooh. Must have been a rough night."

Ray nodded. Tony's visage flashed before him and he shook his head.

"Yeah, something like that."

Eileen made his drink. Usually he would sip it slow while he and Eileen flirted but tonight he didn't feel like it. He downed the drink in one long draw the slammed the glass on the bar.

"Shit!" Eileen said. "Really bad night."

Ray dropped a hundred on the bar then hurried out. He walked around the block to his condo building then buzzed himself in. He went straight to the bathroom, shed his clothes then took a long shower. Afterwards he called Suzette.

"What's up, Ray?" she said.

"Hey baby. Did I wake you?"

Suzette yawned. "No sugar, I was up reading. You okay?"

"Yeah, I'm good. I want to see you tomorrow."

"When?"

"Let's do breakfast."

"I'll be there. I miss you baby."

"Miss you, too."

He placed his smartphone on the dresser then jumped into the bed. After ten minutes scrolling through cable stations he turned off the television then tossed the remote on the chair by the bed.

"That was some freaky shit," he said. After a few fitful starts he finally fell asleep.

Ray jerked up to the morning sun streaming through his blinds. His head throbbed, a sharp stabbing pain that made it hard to see. He stood then almost fell, grabbing the chair for support.

"I didn't drink that much," he said.

He stumbled into the bathroom, filled the sink with cold water then splashed his face. The pain worsened.

"What the hell?" he said.

He looked into the mirror. Instead of seeing his face, he saw the face of Tony Germello

"The hell…!"

He jumped away from the mirror.

"Get yourself together, bruh. Come on now."

He looked into the mirror again. Tony Germello was still there, a victorious smile on his face. The pain spread from his head to the rest of his body. He began to collapse but then caught himself on the sink. As the pain subsided he lost feeling in his feet, then his legs, torso, arms, and his entire body. Tony still looked back with a smile as Ray felt like he was a prisoner in his own head.

"Now that's much better," Tony said. "How you feeling, Ray?"

"I'm crazy," Ray said. "I'm fucking crazy!"

"No, you're not," Tony replied. "You're perfectly fine. At least for now."

"This ain't real!" he said. "I'm asleep. That's it, I'm still asleep."

"I'm afraid not," Tony said. "You're wide awake. A little early for my taste, but appropriate. We got work to do."

Ray watched as Tony rifled through his medicine cabinet for shaving cream and a razor.

"Man, you look like shit," Tony said.

"What the hell you talking about?"

Tony squirted the shaving jell into his hand then lathered his face. Ray noticed that the hands Tony used were his hands.

"See, this is how it works," Tony said. "You see my face, but everyone else sees yours. And they should, because this is your body. I'm just piggy-backing."

"What?"

Tony slid the razor across his cheek.

"See Ray, you fucked up when you looked at me too long. The eyes are the easiest way to get in. Once I'm in it takes a while to get situated. But now it's all good. Once we get cleaned up we'll head out and get this bastard that put the hit out on me. What's his name by the way?"

"What?" Ray said.

"His name? Who's the son of a bitch that put the hit on me?"

Ray hesitated before answering. "I don't know."

A pain like a thousand hot knives rippled through him.

"Listen to me, Ray. You're still here because I want you to be. Keep this shit up and you're gone. Now tell me who put the hit on me."

"I swear, I don't know! Snatch called up then asked me if I wanted to make a grand. Told me to meet him on Ponce."

"You're not shitting me Ray, are you?"

"No, no! I swear I don't know!"

Tony continued shaving. "Looks like the first thing we need to do is pay your boy Snatch a visit."

Tony was finishing his shave when the doorbell rang.

"You expecting company, Ray?"

"Suzette!"

Tony smiled. "Really? As much as I would like to check your girl out we don't have time. I'll make this quick."

"Don't hurt her dammit!" Ray said.

"That's up to her," Tony answered.

Tony opened the door. Suzette posed with her hands on her hips, her tall frame wrapped in a trench coat dress accentuating he ample curves. She'd gone natural since the last time Ray had seen her, shedding her voluminous weave for a simple afro. Ray met her two years ago as she ended her shift at Magic's while he was staking out the club for a target. They hit it off immediately. He talked her into leaving the club life then paid her way through technical school. She was a pharmacy technician now, her former talents reserved just for him.

"Hey baby, you going to let me in?" she said.

"Can't do that," Tony said. "Change of plans. I got some things to take care of."

Suzette sucked her teeth. "And you couldn't call a sister and tell her before I drove all the way over here?"

Tony slipped his arms around Suzette, pulling her close then kissing her. Ray burned. It was like seeing her cheat on him, even though he knew she thought she was kissing him. And she was; except she wasn't.

When they ended Suzette had a big grin on her face.

"Damn, you ain't never kissed me like that!" she said.

"I was inspired," Tony said.

Suzette kissed him again. Ray tried to scream then felt needles of pain.

Tony pushed her away. "You go on home now. I'll call you when I'm done."

Suzette ran her hands over his head. "You hurry up, okay?"

Tony smiled. "I will."

They both watched her saunter away.

"Not bad. Not bad at all."

"Shut the hell up," Ray said.

"If you behave you'll get to see her again. Now let's get busy."

Tony sauntered to the closet then slid open the door.

"Man, you got terrible taste in clothes," he said. "But it ain't like I'm going out on the town."

He selected a pair of jeans, a Falcons sweatshirt and a heavy coat. After dressing he looked in the mirror.

"So, where's Snatch live?" Tony said.

Ray didn't answer.

"Okay, so we do this the hard way."

Ray felt the stabbing pain again.

"Shit! Okay! I'll tell you!"

"No need," Tony said. "I got what I need. See, I got access to everything inside your head. It's just painful for you if I have to go digging. So, let's make this easy, okay? Where are the keys?"

"On my nightstand," Ray said.

Tony picked up the keys, tossed them in the air then caught them.

"Excellent! Let's do this."

They left the condo then went to the parking garage. Ray's 2008 Mustang rested on the fifth level, a hubcap missing.

"What's up with you, Ray?" Tony said. "You don't take care of your body, you don't take care of your ride...I think you got issues."

Ray didn't reply. He was trying to figure a way out.

Tony drove the car recklessly through the parking deck. He barely hesitated at the exit before plunging into morning traffic. They crept to the onramp then merged onto I75/85. Tony took the I75 split at the Brookwood interchange.

"This ain't the way," Ray said

"We have a stop to make first," Tony replied.

Forty-five minutes later Tony took the Cartersville exit. He worked his way through the city until they arrived at an upscale neighborhood nestled in a grove of white oaks. Tony drove up to a two-story brick home near the back of the neighborhood. He was about to exit the car when he slammed his hand against the steering wheel.

"Damn! I don't have my keys! They're with my body."

He looked into the rear-view mirror. Ray saw his face and bit back his words.

"I guess you'll have to break into my house," Tony said. "Ain't that some shit."

He stepped out the car then worked his way around to the back door. He stood for a moment, his hands going to his hips.

"Hmm," Tony said.

"What?" Ray replied.

"I don't remember if I set the alarm."

Tony sauntered to one of the large ceramic plant holders on his patio. He dumped the small bush and soil into the yard then walked back to the house. He threw the plant holder through the window; the alarm went off seconds later.

"I guess I did," Tony said as he shrugged.

He cleared the broken glass and wood, and then crawled in the house.

"Hurry up!" Ray said. "The cops will be here soon!"

Tony took his time climbing the stairs then entered his master bedroom. Ray looked upon the spacious room in awe as Tony amble to the walk-in closet. He shoved his clothes aside to reveal a wall safe.

"Don't look," he said with a smirk.

He punched in the code then opened the door. The safe was filled with money, jewels and guns. Tony went straight to the guns.

"I know what you're thinking," Tony said. "When I'm through with you you'll come back and wipe this place clean. I wouldn't bother if I were you. This is part of the reason you killed me. I'm actually surprised it's still here. I guess they thought since I was dead they had plenty of time to loot my crib."

Tony was inspecting the assault rifle when the doorbell rang. He left the safe and closet then peeked through the blinds.

"The cops are here!" Ray said.

"Let's see what they want," Tony said.

He took his time down the stairs to the front door. Ray tensed as Tony took his time unlocking the door. He hesitated, and then snatched it open. The policeman, a blonde haired middle-aged man, jerked up his head.

"Excuse me sir, I'm Officer Daniels. We had a report of a break in at this house."

"I'm glad you responded so quickly," Tony said. "Come in."

No sooner had the policeman stepped into the door did Tony press his taser into the man's side and pull the trigger. The cop went down immediately in fits and shakes.

"Oh shit!" Ray exclaimed. "You tased a cop!"

"I didn't do a thing," Tony replied. "You did. Now for his friend."

Tony opened the door then waved at the policeman in the car.

"Excuse me officer! Your friend asked me to tell you he needed assistance!"

The officer climbed out the car then hurried inside. Tony tased him to the ground. He returned upstairs to his room safe for duct tape. He returned downstairs then taped the policemen's legs, arms and mouths.

"There," he said. "Now let's go see your friend."

Ray knew better than to hold back; he passed the address to Tony with no protest.

"Cascade Road? I guess killing people pays well."

"Snatch ain't just a killer," Ray said. "He's a facilitator. Anything his bosses' want he's gets. The man is smart."

"He ain't that smart if he's working for the assholes I think he's working for."

"Shoot, the man graduated high school with a 4.0! He could've gone to college if it wasn't for the felony possession charge."

"You're telling me this like I give a shit," Tony said. "All he needs to tell me is who put the hit on me. I'll give him an A for that."

The drive from Tony's to Snatch took about an hour. Ray searched his thoughts, trying to figure out some way to free himself. As they eased up Snatch's steep driveway he was no closer than when they left Tony's mansion.

Tony stuck a Glok in the back of his pants.

"What are you doing?" Ray said.

"Just in case," Tony replied.

"Snatch is cool people," Ray said. "He'll tell you what you want to know."

"See, that's your problem," Tony said. "No one in this business is cool. No one is your friend. All it takes is one order and ol' cool Snatch will be putting a bullet in your head."

Tony climbed the brick steps then banged on the door.

"Hey Snatch! Open up! It's me, Ray!"

They heard Snatch stomping to the door. When he opened it, he was shirtless and sweating.

"Man, you better have a..."

Ray watched in terror as Tony punched Snatch in the gut then struck him across the jaw. Snatch fell immediately. Tony grabbed Snatch under the arms then dragged him inside. Tony took a quick look around.

"Looks like everybody makes more money than you, Ray," he commented.

"Snatch is going to kick your ass when he wakes up," Ray said.

"He's going to kick your ass," Tony said.

Tony dragged Snatch to the nearest chair. He pulled out the Glok then pressed it against Snatch's head. He slapped Snatch lightly on the cheek.

"Wake up Snatch," he said. "I didn't hit you that hard."

Snatch moaned. He attempted to shake his head but felt the gun against it.

"Who paid you do to this?" Snatch managed to say.

"This is a freebee," Tony said. "Who paid you to kill Tony?"

Snatch laughed. "You think I'm going to tell you?"

Tony pulled the gun away from Snatch's head then shot him in the foot. Snatch yelped and grabbed his wounded foot.

"Oh, hell no!" Ray said.

Tony pressed the hot barrel against Snatch's head.

"I'm asking you again," Tony said. "Who paid you to kill Tony?"

"You're dead. You know that, right?" Snatch said.

Tony shot Snatch in the calf. Snatch fell out the chair onto his side and moaned.

"I didn't come here to have a conversation," Tony said. "I'm working my way up to your ass. One more time, who sent you to kill Tony?"

"Low Dog," Snatch said. "Low Dog sent me."

"What?"

For the first time since he entered his head Ray sensed weakness from Tony. Ray pushed at him, feeling his limbs and the Glok in his hand. He had control. He pulled the gun from Snatch's head.

"Snatch! This ain't me doing this to you! Tony took over my mind. He's controlling ..."

Searing pain paralyzed him. Tony shoved him back into his dark space. Snatch had managed to stand and was looking down on them, a .45 in his shaking hand.

"What the hell you talking about, Ray?"

Tony jerked Ray's body out of line sight of Snatch's gun. He shot Snatch twice in the head. Snatch managed to get off a shot as he collapsed to the floor, the bullet grazing Ray's shoulder. Tony stood over Snatch and shot him twice more in the head.

"You killed him!" Ray said.

"Damn right I did," Tony replied. "He killed me, remember?"

Tony forced him to walk out the house and back to the car. In moments they were back on the road, heading north.

"That was some wrong shit," Ray said.

"Shut up," Tony replied.

"You could have kept him alive. He could tell us where to find Low Dog."

"I didn't need him for that," Tony said. "I know exactly where Low Dog is."

Ray felt surprise. Anybody at Low Dog's level kept their whereabouts secret.

"You're lying," he said.

"Shows how much you know. Me and Low Dog came up together. At one time we were closer than brothers. A time came where we both had the chance to move up in the game. Low Dog decided to do it, I didn't."

"You turned down a step up?"

"Yeah. Didn't like the company. Still, me and Low Dog looked out for each other. It was good to have a friend in high places, and it was good for him to have someone close to the streets to keep him current."

"But he sent us to kill you," Ray said.

"Yeah, he did," Tony said. "And I'm going to find out why before I kill him."

They traveled east, through Conyers and beyond Covington. Tony steered the car off I-20 then down a rural two-lane road before turning onto a narrow dirt road bordered by pine trees and blackberry vine laced underbrush. He pulled the car into the brush then went to the trunk and took out his weapons. He inspected the assault rifle as he walked up the trail, and then slipped into the woods. He stayed close to the road until it ended at the edge of a well-groomed yard. The house before them was huge, a French Provencal style stucco home with iron railing trimmed balconies at the upstairs windows. A stretch limo and a green Lamborghini were parked in front, with two guards bordering the front entrance. Tony crept around the perimeter of the home to the rear. Three more guards stood by the rear door, much less attentive than their cohorts in the front. Tony reached into his pocket then pulled out a suppressor. He attached it to the assault rifle's barrel.

"What the hell?" Ray said. "You going in?"

"Yep," Tony said. "I wish you were in better shape. This would be much easier."

"He ain't alone, man!"

"Collateral damage," Tony said.

He raised the assault rifle to this shoulder.

"You going to get us killed!" Ray said.

"I don't care," Tony replied. "I'm already dead."

Tony fired, sweeping the area. When he was done all three guards lay still in the grass. Tony jumped from the brush, running as fast as Ray's body could manage. He was gasping when he reached the rear door.

"I hate your body!" he said.

Tony kicked the door just under the doorknob. The door frame cracked but the door remained closed. He kicked it again and the door flew open. A security alarm activated, the piercing sound causing Ray to wince.

The guards from the front appeared on both sides of the house, their guns drawn. Tony/Ray dove into the house as they opened fire. They rolled onto their back while raising the assault rifle. The first guard charged through the door and Tony riddled him with bullets. The second guard stuck his gun around the door's edge then fired. Tony rolled away as the bullets ripped the floor. He took aim through the window and shot the man twice. He rolled to the floor and stood just in time to see Low Dog running toward the front door in a white warm up suit, his gold chains bouncing against his chest. In his right hand he held a chrome Glok; his left hand gripped the hand of sepia-skinned woman in stretch jeans and a mid-drift top, a look of terror on her face.

"Gotcha," Tony said.

"Don't shoot the girl!" Ray said.

Tony fired. Low Dog let go of the woman's and then clutched the back of his thigh as he fell to one knee. Tony shot the gun from Low Dog's hand. Low Dog fell face first onto the carpeted floor. He rolled onto his back, holding his wounded hand. The woman stood over him, tears running down her cheeks.

"Please don't kill me!" she pleaded.

"Get up against the wall and don't move," Tony ordered.

The woman whined as she did as she was told.

Low Dog glared at them.

"Who the fuck are you?" he said.

"Doesn't matter," Tony replied. "You put a hit on me. You missed."

"I don't even know who you are," Low Dog said.

"Yeah, that's right," he said. "I'm not myself. Still, I'm disappointed in you, Coot."

Low Dog looked puzzled. "Coot? How you know my nickname, nigga?"

Tony smiled through Ray's face. "We grew up together in the SWATS, dog. You telling me you don't recognize you boy Skeet?"

Low Dog's face reflected his shock. "Skeet? You ain't Skeet! Skeet is…"

"Dead?" Tony grinned. "Not quite. But before I kill your ass I need to know why. Why did you put a hit out on me?"

"This shit is crazy," Low Dog said.

Tony shot Low Dog in the shoulder and the woman yelped.

"Who, goddamit!"

"I did, muthafucka!"

Ray felt Tony's presence waver.

“You? You?”

“Yeah, nigga. Me. You were getting soft. Talking all the time about getting out of the game. Some of the bruhs said you were getting cozy with the po-po. It was either you or me.”

“You listened to those assholes? Did it ever occur to you they were trying to break us up? You ever heard of divide and conquer?”

Low Dog seemed contemplative despite the pain in his face.

“Maybe…”

Tony shot Low Dog in the head.

“Maybe it’s too late now, fool,” he said. He looked at the woman cowering against the wall then put the gun to her head. The woman curled up and prayed.

“Don’t do it,” Ray said. “She ain’t got nothing to do with this.”

“So?”

“So don’t do it,” Ray said.

Tony lowered the gun.

“Get the hell out of here,” he said.

The woman scrambled to her feet then fled the house. Tony stumbled to the nearest chair then sat hard.

“This is so fucked up,” he said.

“You done with me now?” Ray asked.

“I should be.”

“Yeah you should be.”

Tony stood then walked to the stairs.

“You know you’re kind of screwed right?”

"What are you talking about?" Ray asked.

"When folks start asking questions about who did this, your name is going to come up sooner or later."

"Soon as you get out of me I'm getting the hell out of the country."

Tony took them to the top of the stairs then walked into Low Dog's gaudy bedroom. He strolled into the bedroom closet then pulled the clothes aside, revealing a large safe.

"You could leave the country…"

He twirled the combination lock about then opened the safe door, revealing stacks of money and jewels.

"Or we can use this investment and start our own thing."

"Will it get you out of me?" Ray asked.

"Eventually," Tony answered.

They found a pillow cover and filled with the money.

"I think we need a drink," Tony said.

"I know just the place," Ray replied.

They returned downstairs. Tony searched Low Dog's body and found his keys.

"By the way, what do you like to drink?" Tony said.

"After a day like today, a Dead Hitler."

"That nasty shit? I see I'm going to have to introduce you to the finer things in life."

They entered the garage. A BMW 750, Audi 8 and Lexus L50 waited. The keys opened the Lexus. They climbed inside then adjusted the seat.

“The finest thing you can introduce me to right now is freedom.”

They started the car then headed down the long driveway.

“All in good time, my man,” Tony replied. “All in good time.”

Of Home and Hearth

By

Kortney Y. Watkins

The room was bright, as befitted a summer day near its close. Beams of gold, yellow, and red sunlight filtered through the glass wall of windows that overlooked the golf course and its lake, which sparkled turquoise and spearmint green. The distant scene of the lonely and equally bold rock called Stone Mountain provided the perfect frame for the vista, which was worthy enough to rival any spread in *Southern Architecture* or *Modern Living*. Smoke Rise, the affluent suburb east of Atlanta boasted the best vantage to see its otherwise hidden enormity and the shameful secret that was hidden from the view of most of Hwy 78: the confederate version of Mt. Rushmore. And even though Stone Mountain Park had long ago choreographed a scene of unity signifying the end of the Civil War in the rainbow colors of its laser light show, from that short distance that boasted just the right angle, the tattoo of confederate pride loomed over the beauty of the area like a sleeping threat. Nevertheless, the beauty of the mountain's surrounding hillsides topped with older homes that couldn't be replicated in quality today and the newer subdivisions which heralded the exclusivity of wealth and generational good Southern breeding would not be denied.

In the Stone house, the dust particles floated lazily in the air, quite content to twinkle in the refracted light and also quite content to annoy the sole occupant of the room with their teasing existence of carefree happiness and worthiness to dwell in the light.

Clay sat down heavily on the hunter-brown leather sectional in the great room and rubbed his temples. He didn't even bother to close his eyes. Open or closed, Hess's look of horror and shock that immediately melted into hurt and disappointment haunted him constantly. *What was I thinking? I wasn't thinking at all though, was I?* He withered, folding in on himself until he lay on the sofa in a fetal position. It was the opposite of manly. But he didn't care. The guilt attacked him at every turn, and he could no longer defend himself.

"It's funny," he mused in muted tones, "I always thought that guilt was an internal experience. Who would've thought that you can sin so deeply that your very skin rejects you?"

As if on cue, the burning, itchy welts began to surface on his forearms again, and he knew that it would only be a matter of moments before they spread all over his body—and that included inconvenient places. They looked like nature's fantastic displays of lightning, and the pain raced along in shattered lines that led to both nowhere and everywhere. His oatmeal skin seared with violent pain with as much energy as Zeus' lightning bolts. Fortunately, he hadn't tested positive for anything, thank God, but the welts were, to his doctor's experienced eyes, unexplainable and untreatable outside of over-the-counter ibuprofen. So, he suffered. *Just as well.*

Sick of being sick, Clay painstakingly unfurled his limbs, sat up, and swayed slightly from the blood rush to his head. He dragged through the great room, cutting through the dining room to get to the kitchen. Clay reached over the many empty bottles of wine and hard liquor that littered the countertop along with numerous food delivery wrappings and piles of crusted, dirty dishes. The rest of the house, with the exception of the bedrooms, was a reflection of the kitchen—mounds of mess everywhere. *But the bedrooms will remain clean,* he had sworn to himself.

He'd only ventured into the master once since the discovery of his indiscretions, and that was to grab some toiletries from the immaculate white and gray marbled master bath and clothes from the custom mahogany walk-in closet. Clay had packed a big bag, sure that Hess would kick him out and that he'd have to take up residence in a Midtown hotel—upscale, of course. But that was not the case. She was the one who did the packing, and along with her toiletries and clothes, took their three kids, the fish, and the family dog. "You don't want your family anymore? You want to live like a bachelor? All right. Enjoy the bachelor life." She had spoken those words with a look of determination in her eyes, careful to get her point across while being equally careful not to upset the children any more than they already were. She was a wise beauty, a protector of home and hearth.

My Hestia. Baby, what have I done!

There was just one more piece of paper on the paper towel roll, and Clay had to snatch what he could from the glue that held it to the obstinate brown paper core. This somewhat successfully accomplished, he reached across the sink to the black and brown speckled granite breakfast bar that served as a divider between kitchen and formal dining room, a recent update.

"Aargh! Son of a biscuit!" he yelled as the open calamine lotion bottle slipped from his unsteady grip and spilled the last bit of its contents into the kitchen sink. Prior to having kids, his mouth was filthier than an eighteenth-century pirate. He took the piece of paper towel and rescued what he could. It wasn't enough. Clay paused. "It wasn't enough. Why wasn't it enough? Everything. I had everything and it still wasn't enough."

Hess wasn't just his queen, she was his goddess. The first time he looked at her it was like seeing the goodness of earth, her skin the color of Georgia clay. He knew she was meant for him. He had smiled hello at the intelligent cocoa eyes that seemed to see him immediately for what he was. But he didn't care. He followed the movement of the light that gleamed and danced around her, noticing how the jet-black curls fell from a high bun in cascades of tendrils. God, how he loved natural hair.

Clay threw the calamine paper towel on the counter. He looked at the clutter and thought about Hess's last words to him. He was indeed living like a bachelor, and that thrill that he found every time he lured in a new girl who loved the swanky cars, the fancy dinners, the staycations and weekend escapes wasn't enough either. That's why one girl turned into two, then two into three, then three into five until he lost the exact count. *The past four years I've seduced what? Fifty girls or more?* His mental inventory became interrupted by the ringing of the house phone.

"That's weird. No one ever calls that number."

He picked up the cordless from the breakfast bar. "Hello."Silence. "Hello?"

"Clay," crackled the voice of Hess. She sounded distant.

"Hess. Baby. I'm so sorry! I don't know what I was thinking. I miss you and the kids. I don't know what I can do to make it up to you, but I swear to God, angel, I'll do anything…anything for us to be together again. I want my family back. I want my family back!" Clay cradled the phone to his ear and began to rock back and forth, a small moan escaping his lips.

"Clay. We miss you too." Hess's voice was rough, almost as if she had a sore throat, and Clay began to get a little concerned.

"Hess. Baby, are you sick? Come home. I'll put the kettle on and make you some hot tea with honey and bourbon. I can run a bath for you too, if you'd like. How's that sound? I'll call Dottie and see if she can come over and watch the kids for us. I can order them a pizza. Jason, for sure, would like that. I'll order Diana and Penelope their favorites too. Just come home. I'll take care of everything else. I swear."

"I know."

"Okay, baby. How long will it take for you to get here? Are you far away? Of course, you are. You're still renting that house in St. Elysia, right? Yeah, of course you are. How stupid of me. I just had Jason's favorite blanket sent there. Did you tell him Daddy misses him? Of course, you didn't. Why would you? I don't deserve that. But when you guys get here, I swear…I swear I'll hold you all in my arms and never let you go. It'll be our family. Together forever."

"I know."

"And Hess, honey, I've learned my lesson. I will never break up our family again or disrespect our bed, our home. Not ever again. Remember when you finally said you'd go out with me? Remember how you told me that against your better judgment you'd give me a try, even though you'd never given anyone else a turn? Remember that? Remember how you said that the only reason was that I was moldable and could be shaped into a good man, since my name is Clay? Remember that? I laughed with you at the table and laughed at you in my head because I thought I knew different. But you were right, angel. You were right. I am nothing without you. This home is nothing without you. It's so cold and it's summer. It's so cold. But I'll let you mold me into being a better man. I swear I will."

"I know."

"Have you gotten the kids yet? Are you getting in the car? How much longer before you get here, baby?"

"Soon." The line went dead and it jolted Clay a bit. She must have been in a place with bad reception, making the call drop. But a small smile crossed his lips, and he let out a shuddering breath at the full realization that his family was coming home.

Clay hung up the cordless and almost knocked over a stack of dishes in the attempt. Another jolt of recognition flung him into a state of awareness, and he looked around the kitchen, then dining room.

"Crap, freaking crap! They can't come home to this mess. They can't."

The next half hour Clay put on the teapot, threw out trash, aired out the house, loaded the dishwasher, and swept the slate and hardwood floors of the downstairs. He glanced at the calamine paper towel and moved it to the other counter near the stove, just next to the olive oil jar. He'd save it as a reminder of everything he'd put himself and his family through. But for now, it needed to be moved out of the way until he could find time to put it in a safe place. Clay couldn't help thinking that he was grateful he'd left the upstairs alone.

Thank you, God! Now to call Dottie.

Dottie, an elderly neighbor who had grown quite fond of the family, particularly the children, was overjoyed about her neighbor's family reunion and agreed to come and watch the kids.

"I'll call you, Ms. Dottie, when the children get here. I'm putting in an online order for pizza, burgers, and chicken tenders as we speak, so don't worry about what the kids are going to eat."

Just then, the doorbell rang and a twinge of excitement, fear, and panic hit Clay all at once. He steeled himself and walked to the front door. On the way, he looked out of the house's picture-perfect window frame to see the stars twinkling in the sky with random red, yellow, and pink streaks and splotches of cosmic *somethingness*. The moon was full and bright. *A harvest moon, I think.* The last window he passed showed his reflection, and he noticed that the ugly, angry storm of pain and suffering had dissipated, though he couldn't recall the moment when that might have been. The adrenaline of anticipation had overshadowed everything else. *Ding-dong,* rang the doorbell again. Clay forgot his reflection and hurried the last few feet to the front door. He opened it wide and all of his family stood before him: beautiful, smiling, and happy.

"Daddy! Daddy! Daddy!" screamed the children, and Clay bent down to hold them close. "We missed you, Daddy!"

"I missed you too, babies. Daddy missed you too." Clay choked back a sob and looked up at his wife. She smiled and he thought there was something different about her. He couldn't be sure, but her favorite scarf appeared to hide a shadow of an ugly line that ran across her neck. A hard tug from Jason snatched away his attention and in the next instant he had forgotten it completely before he could remember to ask if something had happened. Hess cleared her obviously hoarse throat and Clay recalled that his goddess was sick.

"Kids, go on in. Let me get Mommy situated." They ran into the house filling it with much missed laughter. Clay held out his hand tentatively and she took it.

"Angel, you're cold. Let's get you inside and warmed up. I'll take good care of you now."

"I know," she said smilingly. "I forgive you and I believe all of those things that you told me. And I know that our family will be together forever. But Clay, I'm tired. Let's get some sleep. We can sleep near the fireplace in the great room, and the children can sleep with us."

"Are you sure, Hess? I've already called Ms. Dottie, and all we have to do is tell her that we're ready."

"Ms. Dottie's old and has only a few more years left. Let's not bother her."

"Okay, then…if you're sure." Clay raised his eyebrows at her odd statement but shelved it away to a far corner of his mind. The only thing that mattered now was that his home and hearth were once again filled with love and laughter.

Clay and Hess gathered the throw blankets and pillows, stacking them up to make a nest in front of the fireplace, then called the kids so that they could snuggle as a family. Whether it was the sleepless nights, the stress of a broken home, or the recent alcoholic binge from mid-afternoon, Clay fell into the most peaceful, deepest sleep he'd ever remembered.

* * *

"Ms. Dorothy Carr?"

"Yes, that's me."

"I don't know if you remember me, but I'm Fire Inspector Todd Shan."

"Yes, I remember. I've already given you my statement. I don't really want to recall that awful night again. So, if that's what you're here for young man—"

"I just had one more question to go over with you again, if you don't mind, ma'am."

Dottie stared at him in silence, so Todd took it as an opening. "You said that Clayton Stone said that his family was coming over?" Dorothy nodded once. "Huh. Thank you, ma'am."

As Todd turned to walk down the front steps of Dorothy's house, she said, "Why do you find that strange? I can tell that you find that strange."

Inspector Shan wouldn't meet her gaze and looked away, shaking his head at some internal struggle. An impatient clearing of Dottie's throat voiced an insistence that only an elder could command. Shan sighed deeply in submission and leaned forward in a confidential manner.

"Ms. Carr," he said in a subdued voice, just shy of a whisper. "There was only one body found inside the house; it was identified as Clayton Stone, and then there's the fact that Mrs. Stone and her three children were killed in a car wreck earlier that day."

"Are you sure?"

"Quite. The children died upon impact. Mrs. Stone—well, she—she was decapitated by her seat belt." He smiled apologetically, seeing Ms. Carr turn ashen. She was really old, after all.

"Once last thing before you go. How did, you know, the fire start?"

"The darnedest thing," said Shan more to himself than to Dorothy. "Something flammable sat near a tea kettle that got left on, which was next to some kind of cooking oil. Olive oil, we've determined it to be."

My Dinner with Vlad

By

Kyoko M

"Cassandra…why am I staring at a three-foot wooden penis sculpture?"

I grinned. "Welcome to Atlanta, Vlad."

I grabbed his hand and tugged him further into the cacophony of light and color that made up the midtown Atlanta Vortex restaurant. As with every night, the Vortex was packed to burst with people, from trendy twenty-somethings to sedentary elderly folks with great senses of humor. There were several reasons it was one of my favorite spots; great drinks, no kids allowed, insanely delicious and unique burgers, and a widely diverse customer base. The Vortex bore an excellent resemblance to the city around it, honestly. Atlanta was my kind of town. You never stepped out onto those cracked, burning-hot sidewalks and saw the same thing twice.

"Two?" the hostess asked, smiling at me. The smile turned up about seven-hundred watts as she spotted the tall, pale-skinned man behind me. I was used to that reaction. It came with the territory of walking around with the freaking father of all vampires.

"Yes," I said, and my voice snapped her out of what I could tell was a bit of a star-struck trance. I couldn't see him behind me, but the curly hairs springing out from the nape of my neck quivered, meaning he'd sent a bit of glamour her way after he caught that smile she gave him. I squeezed his hand pretty hard and the quivering disappeared, meaning he'd laid off on it.

"This way," she said, a little breathless with slightly wobbly knees, and we followed her to a table in the corner facing the outward window. Dusk had settled over the city. Orange light poured out across the streets and slanted all the shadows sharply to one side.

"Thanks," I said as I sat. Vlad offered the hostess another beaming grin and she flushed a little before scurrying back to the front.

I sent him a sour look. "Really? You whipped it out on the hostess?"

Vlad scowled. "Must you be so crass, my dearest Cassandra?"

I rolled my eyes. "Maybe the giant penis sculpture rubbed off on my vernacular. Sorry. I didn't mean to offend your delicate sensibilities, Fangface."

"Not at all," he purred, lowering his eyelashes over those topaz eyes. "You just gave me a mental image that'll keep me warm Tonight."

"Ha-ha," I said in a dry voice. "How many puns are you going to make before I have to kill you?"

"Probably a thousand or so. You agreed to entertain me Tonight. You should have known better."

The waiter appeared with a bright smile that matched the hostess up front and dropped off our menus. He took our drink orders as well: bourbon for me and a Bloody Mary for the vampire (which he of course thought was hilarious.)

I flipped my menu open and Vlad did the same. "What's good here, my dear?"

"Everything," I said. "Best burgers in Midtown, if you ask me."

"I did ask you." I kicked him in the shin. He laughed that velvety laugh of his and scanned the menu for real this time.

The waiter returned with our drinks and I nursed my bourbon to even me out a little more. My metabolism was insanely high thanks to my size—five foot nine and a solid hundred-and-fifty pounds—and lycanthropes could process food and booze in less than half an hour. My grocery bill was through the roof. It was the only thing I envied the Count for, actually. His diet was a thousand times cheaper, to say the least.

"Do you actually like Bloody Marys or did you really just want to make another awful pun?" I asked around another sip of bourbon.

His eyes twinkled at me over the rim of the glass. "I'm not one to turn down a bloody anything, but in truth tomato juice is good for the body."

I eyed him. "Even dead ones?"

He spread his pale hands. "I didn't get this gorgeous eating doughnuts."

I shook my head. "Did they even have tomato juice when you were alive?"

"Not in handy-dandy bottled form, no, but it was easy enough to get. Waiting for Vodka to be invented was a pain in the ass, though." He drained the glass and licked his lips. You couldn't see his fangs now. Vlad was a shape shifter, among other things. He'd explained to me before that the movies and novels written about his kind exasperated him to no end when they portrayed vampires as constantly having their fangs out. It would make extra work for him when it was time to feed on prey. Sure, he had a hypnotic stare to put weak-willed people under so they'd be compliant, but he was surprisingly progressive for a blood-sucker. Consent was important to him above all. He only fed from willing sexual partners, male and female alike. He was very adamant about it and would punish those of his bloodline who disobeyed the notion. It was one of the few things I actually liked about him.

Admittedly, even without the glamour, he wasn't bad to look at. Not exactly my type—I liked the dark, swarthy fellas—but I didn't mind sitting across from him in the low lights of the Vortex. He was just shy of six-foot-four and had a solid, slim build underneath the black button-up shirt and suit jacket. I'd talked him out of a full suit simply because we were going to a casual place for dinner and it would stand out too much, so he'd instead chosen some comfortable dark-wash Levis and boots to go with it. The first button of the shirt was open, exposing a little triangle of smooth, white flesh that drew the eye line up to his square chin and slender cheekbones.

To me, he looked like a male model that had gotten lost on the way to the set of *Zoolander 3*. Very Alexander Skarsgård-y. He'd glared at me when I told him so and threatened to change into something I'd find more "suitable," but I told him not to. There were a lot of odd things between us, but never an issue of race. I'd seen him in many forms over the years, and he adjusted based on what area he was in and who he would be interacting with, like any smart predator. There were only lingering wives' tales about what he looked like when he was still human. His wife Mina died eons ago, and she would have been the only one who would have a firsthand account. I'd asked him once upfront and he just gave me that mocking smile and asked what I thought he looked like. I'd just rolled my eyes. Vampires hate being straightforward.

Truth be told, I figured he liked the pale, Swedish look if only because he'd lived through times when a white man and a black woman weren't allowed to walk around in public together, romantically linked or not. I didn't fault him for that.

"Are you guys ready to order?" our waiter asked.

"Ladies first," Vlad said, his tone playful.

"I'll go with the Zombie Apocalypse, cooked rare, fries, and a Coke with the meal."

"I'll take Hell's Fury, also cooked rare, fries, and a sweet tea with the meal."

"Excellent. We'll get that out to you shortly." The waiter vanished with our menus.

Vlad set his chin on a long-fingered hand and stared at me. I stared back. It may or may not have been a miniature contest.

"You're taller than I remember," he said quietly after a while. "Did that happen recently?"

"No," I said. "I'm wearing boots, remember?"

"Ah."

"That, or your memory's going, old man."

He narrowed his eyes at me. Vlad was vain at times. "Age before beauty, little girl."

"Beauty?" I snorted. "When did that happen?"

He reached out and tugged at one of my curls, his lips forming a satisfied smirk. "You aren't the awkward little puppy I met all those years ago. You've blossomed rather nicely, I'd say."

As if I needed a reminder. I'd been a beanpole from childhood to my teenage years with nary a curve in sight. Then, I hit twenty-one, and poof! The breast-and-ass fairy was summoned from seemingly out of nowhere. Though, I should note fairies hate that metaphor and will curse you if they hear you say it. My mother told me she was the same way, so it was probably just genetic, like our shared lycanthropy. I'd also inherited her curly mop of dark brown hair that neither of us ever wanted to tame. Today, I'd smoothed it back into a soft white elastic band that matched my t-shirt and contrasted the black jeans and boots. I guiltily admit to wearing a bit of makeup, mostly so the Count wouldn't outshine me in the attractiveness department. Competitive? Who? Me? Naaaaaah.

Fangface had been around since I was in my early teens. He stayed overseas for the most part, taking care of his clan and enforcing the various laws in his domain, and he vacationed in America every so often when there were important supernatural gatherings. I distinctly remembered feeling nervous as I opened the front door and he stood on the porch with that penetrating gaze and that wolfish grin, his eyes twinkling as he asked me, "Aren't you going to invite me in, Cassandra?"

"Right," I'd gulped. "Please do come in, Count."

He'd chuckled and stepped inside, patting the top of my head fondly. "I'm only teasing. It's lovely to meet you in person finally, sweet Cassandra."

I'd nodded, my mouth still a bit dry. I couldn't be blamed for being nervous. The guy had drained an allegedly two million people in his lifetime. "Nice to meet you."

He'd lifted my hand and kissed it. "Nice to meet you. Call me Vlad."

I snapped back to the present, wrinkling my nose at his wording. "You do realize my parents would tear you in half if they heard you say that. Also, it's gross. Extra, extra gross. You sound like Edward Cullen."

Snap. I glanced down to see a literal crack in the wooden table where his other hand rested along the side of it.

He sent me a hateful glare. "You know how much I *hate* that pathetic sop of a fictional character, Cassandra. Do not spoil my evening."

I held up a hand. "Alright, fine, low blow. But my point still stands."

"I'm trying to compliment you. I hear young women like that sort of thing."

"Thanks, but I'm good. I don't need compliments from He Who Conquers. You're not going to rustle my jimmies, Fangface."

He laughed that rich laugh again. The light overhead flickered just a tad and my hackles rose. He could use that voice like a weapon if he felt like it, and it was still unnerving to me. He hadn't done it on purpose. Alcohol makes it harder for him to control his impulses.

"Is that what they're calling it these days?" he mused, reaching for my bourbon. I let him take a sip. Dead guys don't have cooties, after all.

"That's what I call it, anyway."

"You sound like your father. I think he said something similar the first time he met your mother."

I shuddered. "Did not need to know that."

"Why not? I think they had a terribly romantic first encounter."

"In the middle of a war to free the slaves in Egypt?" I asked, crossing my arms over my chest. "Sure, I can write the next great American romance novel about it."

He lowered the bourbon, licking his soft lips once more. *Dammit, Cassandra, focus.* "Nonsense, my dear. Meeting a mate amidst battle is an unforgettable experience. There's nothing more thrilling than seeing your equal on the field. Are you telling me you've never done such a thing in your pack?"

"Not exactly," I said, taking my drink back and draining it. "Mind you, it's not slim pickings down here in Atlanta. There's no shortage of hot guys in my pack but being the original Wolfman's daughter kind of puts caution tape around me. They wouldn't touch me with a thirty-nine-and-a-half-foot pole."

The amusement slipped from his handsome features. "Sounds lonely."

I shrugged. "You get used to it. I'm not in a hurry. I'm twenty-eight. I'm barely into my lifespan. There'll be time for romance later."

"Time," he said softly. "Is an illusion. It passes faster than you think, my dear."

I sighed. "What do I have to do to get you to stop calling me that?"

The mad twinkle in his eyes returned. "I can think of a few things."

I groaned. Walked right into that one. "Are you always like this?"

He sat back in the booth, stretching his long arms out and still fixing me with that stare that made my stomach do a few backhand springs. Stupid stomach. "No."

I narrowed my eyes at him. "What's your plan here, Vlad? Do you really think I'm gonna fall for this? It's not like I don't know any better."

"I don't know what you're talking about, my dear Cassandra," he drawled, lazily drawing his gaze from my ponytail down to my throat. I should have worn a turtleneck. Too bad it was summertime or I would have.

Thankfully, the burgers came out a moment later and we both tucked in. He couldn't flirt with me if his mouth was full, after all.

We finished our meal, had another round of drinks, and left. The hostess slipped him her number on the way out. I thought my eyes were going to roll out of my skull and onto the concrete sidewalk.

"That," Vlad said, rubbing his (toned, flat, utterly tempting—dammit, Cassandra!) stomach as we walked. "Was delicious. I commend you for your choice. I'm really getting a good sense of the city. I see why you chose to make this your home. It suits you."

"Does it?" I asked, checking my watch.

"Yes. It's bustling and vibrant. Everyone is different. There's art and beauty and complications everywhere. Not like home in Transylvania. I'm enjoying it."

"Good," I said, and genuinely meant it. "But the night life's just getting started."

He faced me. "I see. Did you have something in particular in mind, my dear?"

I bared my teeth. "As a matter of fact, I do. This way, my dear Count."

He offered me a mock bow and followed me. We walked several blocks. I didn't tell him where we were going on purpose. I wanted to see his reaction.

By the time we stopped in a blind alley, the sun had already set and the darkness had painted over the streets and buildings of Midtown with its long brushstrokes. I'd found somewhere that the orange-yellow streetlamps couldn't light properly. Shadows were a girl's best friend when she was what I was, after all.

"Cassandra," Vlad said evenly. "Are you planning to murder me and steal my wallet?"

I laughed. "Like you've got any money on you."

"Point taken. Even so, I have to say I'm not sure what you're getting at—"

He stopped in mid-sentence as I turned and took off my leather jacket. I dropped it on the cleanest spot I could find on the sidewalk and undid the belt to my jeans. Vlad eyed me as I removed my shirt next.

"Cassandra," he said, his voice pitched much lower this time. "What are you doing?"

"Isn't it obvious?" I asked in my most innocent voice, unzipping my jeans.

Vlad's breathing elevated after the boots and jeans came off. He stood perfectly still; his hands open at his sides, and the lack of lighting left most of his face in shadow…except for his eyes. They glittered at me like jewels. I had to admit I sort of liked the way he was looking at me. Not that it was smart, mind you. I'd seen the wolves in my pack look at deer this way. Still, there is a kind of thrill one gets from being face to face with a predator—a delirious, insane, pleasurable thrill from danger that anyone and anything with a pulse can't deny.

His gaze tugged upward as I reached into my hair and undid the ponytail, letting dark brown curls cascade down around my cheeks and neck. His eyes kept going down and down and down over my chocolate skin one inch at a time, and my body couldn't help but flush in response to the open, naked hunger on his features. He hadn't moved a muscle, but I could tell he was struggling to remain a rational person and not give into the monster beneath that alluring surface.

But I wanted the monster Tonight.

I stepped towards him in just my bra and panties, deliberately slow, rolling my hips with every step, my eyes never leaving his. "What are you waiting for?"

He seemed to struggle to speak. "My dear, I cannot be held accountable for what happens if you come any closer."

I gripped the front of his suit jacket and grinned up at him as I undid the buttons. “Get your mind out of the gutter, Fangface. We’re going for a run.”

Vlad exhaled deeply in relief and then glared at me. “That. Is *not*. Funny.”

I batted my eyelashes at him. “No, it’s hilarious.”

“Bloody hell, you millennials,” he spat, shrugging out of the suit jacket and throwing it on the ground. “You think everything’s a joke, don’t you?”

I shrugged. “Couldn’t resist. You’re so unflappable. I wanted to flap you.”

He caught my wrist and tugged me close, up against the wall of muscle that was his chest and abs, and with nearly nothing on, the sensation was…indescribable. He smiled and lowered his voice, using a little glamour to make it tickle along my skin and in my ears.

“That can be arranged, my dear.”

I didn’t gulp. Wouldn’t give him the satisfaction. Instead, I gave him my best poker face and answered in total deadpan, “Flap you.”

Vlad laughed again. God, did it feel good. Stupid vampire. “Touché.”

He let me go and finished undressing until he was just in his boxer briefs, folding his clothes neatly and dropping them next to mine.

I twirled my finger. “Turn around.”

He widened his eyes to look innocent. “Why, Cassandra, I’m hurt that you felt the need to say that to me. I’m a perfect gentleman. I’d never dream of…”

He let his eyes rove over my half-naked body again. "…sneaking a peek."

"You say that," I said mildly, and then let my own eyes wander below his waistline. "And yet somehow I don't believe you."

Vlad grinned damn near hard enough to split his cheeks in half. "Pardon me. I wasn't lying when I said you've blossomed."

Trust the vampire to be completely unashamed about his own arousal. Figures. "Turn around before I bite your arm off."

He clucked his tongue. "Such trust issues you have, my dear."

He obeyed. I gave it a second or two and then dropped my lingerie. It was cool out, a fact I was quite grateful for, and the moon hung like a silver coin in the cloudy night sky. I reached deep inside me for that warm nest of power and changed into a wolf.

It was difficult to describe the way it felt when I changed. It didn't hurt…but it didn't *not* hurt. I'd once told a friend that it was like peeling off a fingernail where most of the skin wasn't attached and so you didn't bleed. My muscles shifted around. My bones popped and cracked as they rearranged into the lithe, streamlined form of a wolf that stood perhaps half a foot taller and several pounds heavier than a real one. When I was within the city limits, I always went with my full wolf form. I could switch to a form between the two that was bipedal—the kind that normal people wrote into movies like

Van Helsing or the Benicio del Toro remake—but if anyone caught sight of me, that would be that. Supernatural folks stayed under the radar, if only because humans are ruled by fear and panic, and to know that a cute black girl could turn into something that could tear them apart in just the blink of an eye would induce instantly genocide on our kind.

My fur was dark-brown, matching the color of my skin, and my mane had black streaks running through it and along my spine, ending in a tuft at my tail. A shudder spilled through me once the transformation was done and I shook out my fur, getting used to the change in senses. I could smell who had been in this alley within the last four days. I could hear the kids playing basketball four blocks away. I could taste the vile air coming off the dumpster nearby. I could see through the veil of darkness draped over the city as if it were broad daylight.

Being a wolf is where it's at, man.

Vlad turned around and smiled warmly at me. "Such a pretty thing. I'd forgotten."

I rolled my-now-golden eyes and he chuckled before following my lead. He turned away and rid himself of the boxer shorts.

Vlad's transformation was smoother and faster than my own. He just sort of…*melted* into a puddle of dark mass and then reformed into a black-furred wolf slightly taller than me, but not as bulky with muscle, with startling arctic blue eyes. He walked over and sniffed me a bit, then nuzzled me, his shoulder bumping mine playfully. I heard his voice in my head as clear as day even though his fanged jaws never moved.

Where are we off to, my dear?

Follow me, I replied. *Stay close. People are jumpy around this area and you don't want someone to pop a cap in your furry ass.*

He laughed in my head as I broke into a sprint further down the alley.

Midtown Atlanta's nightlife was delightful. I loved it. Music pounded through the buildings, whether just a private citizen jamming in their little studio apartment or a live band in a local dive bar getting it in for the night. I could smell every dish from fine dining restaurants wafting out through their front doors as new customers walked in. I could hear people on their first dates walking towards their cars, laughing nervously and flirting. I could see the cars rushing back and forth over the potholes, honking and screeching and filling the air with noise.

Life. That was what I liked about Atlanta. Life happened. It never slept.

Despite my large size, I darted in and out of the streets because I'd been doing it all my life. When I was young, my father took me to Fourth Ward Park and taught me how to change at will, safely and quietly where no one would be looking for us in the middle of the night. Once I learned how to operate outside of the humans' normal senses, it was easy to get around town without being seen or be seen so little that people could talk themselves into thinking I was simply a large breed of dog.

Vlad kept up with me without breaking a sweat. He too was an expert at stealth, though he didn't use his wolf form as much as I did. Over the years, I'd seen most of his favorite forms: a hawk, a serpent, a cat, and even one time on a bet, a bat. He enjoyed being in his human form the most simply because he liked the challenge of seducing his prey, but he had admitted to me before that in animal form, he could be unrestrained. He could run or jump as fast as he wished to go, whereas in human form people would raise eyebrows at a man who could leap forty-feet straight up into the air or flip a car with one flick of his wrist.

For once, I let myself have fun. I poured on my agility until I was going fast enough that Vlad caught onto what I was doing. We had reached a neighborhood with a long straightaway and so the two of us raced each other, seeing who could hit the Stop sign at the end of the street faster. All I could hear was our claws scraping the street and the constant panting from our muzzles as we sprinted.

I skidded to a stop and let my tail whack the metal pole of the Stop sign, my mouth wide open in a victorious wolfish grin, no pun intended.

Too slow, Count, I teased.

Please, he said. *I let you win.*

Bullshit.

Is that so? He asked haughtily. *Perhaps you'd like a rematch?*

Perhaps I would, old man.

He eyed me with those glacial irises. *What do I get if I win?*

Bragging rights.

Vlad huffed in disappointment. *Boring.*

What did you have in mind, then?

He cocked his head to one side. *I get to ask you any question I wish and you have to answer it truthfully.*

I eyed him. *And what do I get if I win?*

I'll buy the next round of drinks after we're done.

I thought it over. I actually wouldn't mind another bourbon. It's expensive to get sauced when you're a werewolf. *Deal.*

Vlad nodded his furry head towards the Stop sign another fifty yards away straight ahead. *On your mark, my dear.*

We lined our paws up against the white paint on the street. *On three?* I asked.

Vlad nodded again.

Three!

I booked it. My paws barely touched the street. I might as well have been flying. He vanished from my side as I let loose and just hauled ass down the street, the houses blurring past as if I had rocket boots on. *Eat my dust, old man!*

When I was about ten feet from the stop sign, Vlad simply…*appeared.*

I had to slam my back paws into the ground to keep from colliding with him. The tall black wolf sat at the finish line with a smug, knowing look across his muzzle and I stopped just short of bumping into his furred chest. Our wet noses brushed each other and Vlad's supremely smug voice spoke in my head.

Who are you calling old man, little girl?

I glared. *Show off.*

He chuckled. *Sore loser.*

Whatever, Fangface. What's your stupid question?

He stared into my eyes for a while and his voice came out gentle. *What is the real reason why you don't have a mate?*

I stilled. *Seriously?*

Seriously.

His voice was utterly sincere. It sounded weird. Vlad was probably the least sincere person I'd ever met. He constantly hid behind his charm. He wanted everyone to think he was a perfect, godly being with zero flaws. I hadn't seen him ever really care about anyone except for my parents. They'd been friends for longer than I'd been alive. He'd come to town with the intention of a reunion, but my parents got called away to Savannah to help another pack that was warring with some rogue werewolves. I offered to take him around to sight-see until they came back in a few days. He and I always had a weird sort of relationship; the kind some people had with friends of the family. He was friendly with me, always teasing, always trying to impress me or make me laugh.

He knew me, to some degree, but we hadn't exactly had any heart-to-heart conversations over the years.

Why do you want to know? I asked finally, my tail swishing nervously behind me.

Your parents worry about you. They tell me that isolation isn't good for a pack member. It can cause problems in the ranks after a certain point. Instability.

It took me a second to reply. *Tell me that's not the reason you're here.*

Vlad licked his chops. *Cassandra...*

Holy hell, I groaned. *My parents want you to mentor me.*

Not precisely. They just...wanted me to have a word with you.

Why? I demanded. *Remember the whole 'He Who Conquers' title? You're a player, Vlad. What, are you supposed to give me a playbook on how to catch a man?*

He stood then and loomed over me, his eyes flashing. *Careful. I don't care for your tone.*

I don't give a shit, I snapped back. *What makes you think I even want a mate? And what makes you think I'd take any advice from you to begin with?*

What happens every year during mating season, Cassandra?

I blinked at him. *Excuse me?*

You go on a cruise. Every year. You spend the entire mating season thousands of miles away from the nearest viable mate. Now tell me why that is?

I growled at him. *None of your business.*

You, he continued as if I hadn't said anything. *Are afraid of being vulnerable. You are afraid that finding yourself a mate will change you. You're fiercely independent and you think that finding a mate means you'll be some alpha's literal bitch for all eternity.*

I bared my fangs at him. *Watch your mouth, old man.*

That, he said firmly. *Will not happen.*

I hesitated. *What?*

Your fear of being overrun or controlled by an alpha is unfounded. That's not how a pack works. It's about balance, not conquest. You don't need to run away from that, Cassandra. Opening yourself up to someone doesn't mean you become their slave.

How would you know?

I'm your father's best friend. I've watched him rule the pack for centuries. I know the inner workings of pack courtship better than any other vampire on this earth.

I cocked my head to one side. *Are you saying you've been with werewolves before?*

He coughed slightly. *Not in the way that you're thinking, but yes. I've chosen a mate or two here and there. It's not against pack law to date a vampire, after all.*

Good to know, I said sarcastically. I sighed. *Fine. I'm sorry I snapped at you. I like being on my own. I don't...know how to be any other way. Maybe it's not good for me. I can admit that.*

A wise admission, Vlad said, standing up and stretching his back legs. *All I want is for you to think it over.*

We all want what is best for you. It would be a shame for a woman as smart and charming as you to be alone.

I couldn't blush in wolf form, but the comment warmed my fur quite a bit. *Shut up, you damn flirt.*

He let out a happy little bark; his version of a laugh. *Never.*

A chorus of howls broke through the formerly pleasant atmosphere.

Vlad's head snapped around toward the wall of darkness facing the woods behind the small cul-de-sac ahead of us. *What was that?*

I narrowed my eyes. *Curtain call.*

He glanced sharply at me. *What?*

Just follow my lead, I said, stepping forward into the circlet of houses at the end of the block.

Leaves rustled. Twigs cracked. Heavy breaths broke through the darkness. A half dozen pair of eyes lit up in the shadows, bobbing and weaving as they moved closer. The street lamps had died long ago and hadn't been replaced, hiding the entire area from the human eye.

A wolf pack stepped out of the yard of a nice little two-level house. Three grey, two black, and one brown wolf. The brown wolf stood at the front of the formation and blinked empty yellow eyes at me and Vlad.

Evening, he said in a clear, arrogant voice. *Out for a midnight stroll, your highness?*

The other wolves sniggered as I narrowed my eyes at the ringleader. *Needed some fresh air. Your ego has been clogging up the city over the last week. I can't stand the stench.*

The brown wolf lowered his head slightly. *Mind running that by me again, your highness?*

You heard me, shitstain.

The brown wolf licked his chops. *I don't like your tone, sweetie pie.*

Tough shit.

His lip curled back from his fangs. *I take it that's a no to my offer, then?*

You can cram your offer up your mangy ass, Frederick. Now get off my land and take your buzzards with you.

Vlad stepped up next to me, nudging my shoulder, his voice strained. *Cassandra, what are you doing?*

My job, I spat.

Cassandra, he said sharply. *Explain yourself.*

Oh, it's pretty easy to explain, Frederick said, stalking forward. His buddies flanked him on either side. *I've been considering a change in management for the city of Atlanta. Her parents haven't been here for more than a week and they left the little honeypot in charge. I thought she might not be up to the task, so I suggested that she become my mate and we split the responsibility.*

Bullshit, I said. *You wouldn't stop there. I'm not dumb. I know as soon as my back is turned, you'll kill me and then my parents after you get their trust.*

He snorted. *I'm hurt, your highness. I'd at least have the decency to screw you senseless before I ripped your throat out. From what I hear, you could use a good screw.*

Vlad lowered his head and let out an impressive growl, his jaws parting to reveal long, sharp white fangs. *Mind your tongue, mortal, or I'll rip it from your skull.*

Who is this prick? Frederick laughed. *Is that why you came Tonight? To teach us a lesson with your big buck backing you up? You think that'll stop us from tearing you to pieces?*

I guess we'll find out, won't we? I answered.

Goddamn it, Cassie! Vlad snarled at me. *What have you gotten me into?*

I couldn't answer him. The pack attacked.

The pack split—two grey wolves pounced for me from the front, the one black wolf from the right side, and the others went after Vlad. I knew this formation. I'd done it enough times when I went out with my pack to hunt deer for practice.

I backpedaled as their jaws snapped at my front legs. They missed by mere inches. I slashed a paw at the black one's head and it knocked him aside, throwing him off-balance. The other two darted in again and I spun, lashing both back paws at their snouts. It connected and they both let out yelps of anger and pain.

I whirled and bit into the black wolf's mane, dragging him hard to one side and slamming him into one grey wolf. They landed in a pile a few feet away, momentarily dazed, which gave me a few more precious seconds. The other grey wolf bit me in the shoulder. Pain lanced through my side all the way down to my ribs. I roared and took a chunk out of his front right leg and he let go, stumbling.

His body bubbled and grew in size, his torso stretching into the shape of a man's chest, his hind legs still the same shape but longer as he stretched into his wolfman form. The wolves behind him followed suit, and so did I. My claws grew long and sharp as fingers pushed through the rounded paws and I leapt into the air over their heads, disappearing into the safety of the forest behind the house.

I raced between the trees as the wolfmen came stomping after me. The closest one was on my left flank. I waited until he lunged and swept out a clawed foot, raking it across his eye. He shrieked and crumpled to the ground, clutching his face.

The other two closed in. I snatched a fallen log and hefted it at the one closest to me. He swiped it aside, but the moss and dirt scattered in a cloud around his face. I slashed one side of his face open, clipping off one ear. He roared and collapsed to one knee, bleeding profusely.

The other wolf tackled me. I slammed into the loam and leaves of the forest, gasping as it drove the air from my lungs. He reached for my throat, but I rolled to one side so that he got a handful of dirt instead. I kicked him in the midsection once, twice, hearing his ribs crack, but he didn't move an inch. He snapped at my face with his fangs and I held him off me with my legs, struggling to breathe again to gather my strength. His teeth sunk into my shoulder and I howled in pain, sinking my claws into his shoulder blades and shredding them. He let go and tried to claw at my head again, but I ducked and used every ounce of power I had left in me to throw him off. He landed hard a few feet away and rolled back into a crouch. By the time he'd gotten his feet beneath him, I'd already leapt through the air.

I tore his head off in one messy swipe of my claws.

The head rolled several yards and came to a stop at the bottom of the hill. I stood there, panting heavily, bleeding in several spots, adrenaline making every sight and sound sharp in my senses. I could hear the other two were on their feet, but when I turned, they were staring at me and at the headless corpse at my feet.

Who else wants some? I snarled.

The other two whimpered and shrank back in a flinch. They went back into their full wolf forms and disappeared into the woods in the opposite direction. Good riddance.

I raced back to the cul-de-sac in my full wolf form. Vlad had the other black wolf holding onto his tail to keep him in place while the others circled, trying to find a vulnerable spot to bite. I launched myself into the air and slammed my entire body into the black wolf, paws first. I heard his neck snap and he went limp on the pavement. Like the corpse in the woods, his body shrank back into its nude human form. I landed behind Vlad facing the other way so that we were back to back.

Are you alright? He asked in a low, angry voice.

Still breathing, I said. *You?*

He didn't answer, as Frederick chose that moment to speak. *Looks like the bitch got lucky after all. No matter. You'll get to die by your mate's side instead.*

Vlad let out a dry chuckle. *She should be so lucky.*

I tossed a glare in his direction. *Asshole.*

Gentlemen, Vlad said smoothly. *I'm going to give you precisely one chance to apologize to my friend. If you choose to do so, I will make your deaths quick and painless. If you don't, you'll die screaming and in considerable agony. Choose.*

Frederick let out another humorless laugh. *Where did you find this guy?*

I couldn't grin, but I came pretty close. *Transylvania.*

Frederick and the remaining pack members froze. *What did you say?*

Vlad chose that exact moment to transform.

Vampires are funny things. They can take on all kinds of forms, both human and animal alike, but they aren't limited to that. No one really knows where Vlad came from or what the extent of his powers are because he has never let anyone see them all at once. I'd heard old wives' tales that he was a demon that got kicked out of hell and that was why he had so many abilities, why he fed on human blood, why he lurked in darkness and disliked sunlight. No one but him knew just what he could do, but they knew not to piss him off or they'd find out.

Frederick and his buddies were about to find out.

Vlad's body stretched up from the wolf form into a mostly human shape. His lower body simply wasn't there. It was a mass of shadows with a naked male torso that had one human arm and something that I couldn't really describe at first glance. My eyes adjusted and put together the shape his right arm had made. Vlad was a big fan of irony.

His entire right arm had formed the head of an enormous black wolf.

A wolf's head the size of a freaking pickup truck.

The wolves started shaking from head to toe, their ears flat to their heads, their tails curled against their hindquarters. Frederick actually pissed himself as he stared wide-eyed at the monster before him.

Gentlemen, Vlad said in a deathly quiet tone. *You chose poorly.*

The two wolves behind Frederick bolted. They were fast. I wouldn't have been able to catch them.

But Vlad did.

The pavement in front of the wolves turned black and their paws sunk into it as if they had been in quicksand. They yelped in fear and thrashed madly, yowling as they disappeared into what looked like a void of some sort. They vanished with pained screams and then the road turned back into its normal grayish stone.

Frederick wasn't so lucky.

Vlad faced him and a cold smile touched his lips. *Little pig, little pig, let me in.*

He took a step forward, continuing the rhyme. *Not by the hairs on my chinny-chin-chin.*

He took another step towards the wolf frozen in fear before him. *Then I'll huff and I'll puff and I'll blow your house in.*

He ate Frederick in one clean bite.

Holy shit.

Vlad's shadowy form shrunk down until he resumed his wolf body. He turned slowly and stared at me with pure fury in his eyes. *You.*

I wish I could say that I stood there, proud and tall, while staring a monster in the face.

I fled.

The city blurred past my vision. I ran without thinking, because I knew my city. I knew every turn, every street corner, every alleyway, every sidewalk and catwalk. I didn't need sight. I could feel it around me. For that reason, I made it back to the alley where I'd left my clothes in about three and a half minutes.

But Vlad was already waiting for me.

I had just changed back into my human form when I felt two large hands with steely fingers grasp my wrists hard and then he slammed me into the brick wall behind me. He pinned me there by my arms and slid his knee between my legs so I couldn't run away.

"What. The. Hell. Were. You. *Thinking?*" Vladimir Tepes, Vlad the Impaler, The Count, He Who Conquers, Dracula, Lord of Darkness growled in my face from inches away.

I held perfectly still. Probably not a good idea. I looked like prey right now, and he was so angry that I could see his incisors poking out from beneath his upper lip. His blue eyes blazed with unbridled fury and felt like they were scorching holes into my skull.

I licked my lips and tried to slow my breathing. It didn't work. I was gasping for air and trembling all over. "I didn't know what else to do."

"You didn't know what else to do," he repeated, disbelief thick in his tone. "You expect me to believe that, Cassandra Victoria Moody?"

I shuddered as he used my full name. Supernatural creatures had a lot of magic flowing through them and one of those kinds of magic was attached to a person's full name. It hit me like a slap in the face. I couldn't breathe for a few seconds.

"The pack wouldn't act after I told them about the threat he made. Frederick is new blood from San An-Tonyo. He's a spoiled pretty boy with good breeding, so everyone believed him over me. They said I was just being paranoid and difficult. My parents told me to let it ride, that he wouldn't be stupid enough to actually try anything. I knew they'd be here again after he made that proposition last night. I figured it would be easy for you to—"

"To what?" he demanded. "Kill them before they tried to kill me?"

"Vlad, you were in no real danger—"

"But you were!" he roared, squeezing my wrists. "You risked your life over this without having the common decency to warn me. Why?"

"I didn't know if you'd help me!" I yelled. "What other choice did I have?"

He fell silent, staring into my eyes. "I would have believed you, Cassandra."

It hurt to meet his gaze now. I glanced aside. "I didn't know that."

"You should have," he whispered. "I would do anything to protect you."

He let go of my right arm and touched my face, turning it towards his. He slid his fingers down my chin to wrap around my throat, holding me there while he hovered inches away, his pale eyes suddenly soft and deep. I realized how close we were standing, how heavily we were both breathing, how the whole world seemed to fall away when he was looking down at me like that. Maybe I did know him better than I thought.

"How badly are you hurt?" he asked quietly.

I shook my head a little. "Shallow wounds. They'll heal in less than an hour."

He exhaled and licked his lips, his eyes lowering towards the blood splattered over my shoulders, my neck…and most of all, my breasts. My pulse skyrocketed. His skin was warm from having fed recently, and the way we were pressed together let me feel pretty much all of him. He was very, very pleased with the proximity of my naked body. I admittedly didn't mind his all that much either, and that meant we were both in serious trouble.

"Cassandra," he murmured. "I must admit that I owe you an apology."

"For what?"

His eyes glowed. "I peeked."

I met his gaze and then smiled slowly. "So did I. You've got a nice ass for a dead guy."

Apparently, that was all the consent he needed. He leaned those few inches across my upper body and kissed me.

Good God, sweet Mary and Joseph.

I hadn't ever kissed a vampire before. In essence, vampires were succubi. They fed on blood and lust and that was what made them function, gave them energy, and provided them with the magic to do that voodoo they did do. So part of me knew that what I felt was because of his magic, his life force, his abilities.

But damn did he know how to kiss a gal.

His lips felt impossibly soft on mine. My mind exploded. I couldn't think straight. Pure heat enveloped my body and splashed over every single corner of it. Utter pleasure doused me from head to toe. This was it. This was the living embodiment of ecstasy. Who cared if he decided to devour me whole? It would've been worth it just because of this kiss.

Vlad groaned deeply and sweetly in the back of his throat and the vibration from that delicious sound tickled down the front of my body. He licked my lips enough to part them and kissed me again, burying his other hand in my hair so that I'd tilt my head back. My tongue swept over the inside of his mouth and I felt his fangs for a second, carefully maneuvering around them. I didn't remember winding my arms around his neck, but at some point, I did because I could feel the sheer power and definition in his shoulders and back muscles. I felt the solid heat of his chest and abs and the undeniable proof that he wanted me right here, right now, despite all the ridiculous reasons why that was an incredibly bad idea.

"This is so wrong," Vlad murmured, biting my lower lip gently, not enough to break skin. "Had my soul not already been damned, it would be now."

I nodded in agreement, my voice vacant. "Yup. Mine too."

He smiled a little and managed to pull away just enough to ask, "Worth it?"

"So freaking worth it."

He laughed softly and slid his hand down from my hair to settle on the small of my back. It felt heavenly. He traced the shape of my lips with his thumb. "We should go."

"Yeah," I mumbled. "We are two naked people standing in the middle of an alley making out while covered in blood. Not exactly inconspicuous."

"Indeed. Can you control yourself long enough to get dressed?"

I arched an eyebrow. "Hey, you kissed *me*, pal."

"A fact I shall never live down, mostly because your parents will kill me if they ever find out about it," he lamented. And yet he didn't stop rubbing the small of my back with those long, talented fingers.

"My lips are sealed."

He took my cue and kissed me again, slowly, softly. "So they are."

"So do you forgive me?"

Vlad squinted at me. I sweated it out for a moment, but then he nodded. Relief flooded through me and made it a little easier to apologize. "I'm sorry. I should have trusted you."

"Now you know better," he said. "I will always protect you. I will always come when you call. I am not mate material, nor will I ever be it, but maybe, someday, we can find out where this might lead."

I felt a smile curl across my lips. "Sure. Maybe in another three hundred years, my parents won't find the idea repulsive."

He laughed as he let me go. "Let's call it five hundred, my dear."

I winked at him as I reached for my clothes. "Tempus fugit."

Not Your (Magical) Negro

By

M. Haynes

The lights turn on and all of us squint to see our possibilities for the night. Mine is tall brown skinned trade in a Falcons fitted, a red shirt, and black jeans. He smiles at me and finally takes his hands off my hips. He has all of his teeth and none of them are gold. Good so far.

"So, where we going?" He asks me. He thinks he's slick.

"I thought about going to the after-hours, but what you up for?" I say back. He could be fun. We start walking to the back door to take the exit through the patio. The female security guards guide all of us outside, laughing and joking with the ones who had too much to drink to get out by themselves.

"Where's your place?" He asks. He walked in front of me down the stairs and looks back at me. I can tell he hopes it's close.

"West End," I say. "Bout fifteen minutes from here."

"Ok cool. Gimme your address and I'll meet you at your house."

By this time, we were on Peachtree in front of Bulldogs. I stop and look up at him, letting the chatty group of friends behind us pass us by. "Nah bruh. You can get in the car and ride." My best friend's voice screamed in my head: "Don't you let no one night man get your address saved! You'll fuck around and he'll be done moved in before you put the sheets back on your bed!"

Luckily, he shrugs. "Cool with me. You gone bring me back to my car?" We start back walking towards where I parked.

"If you're good," I flirt. I remembered the last nigga that came over. I made him call an Uber back to his own car because he wasted my time. We crossed the street to Peachtree Place and the credit union where my car is parked. We have to move in between the drunk queens bucking in the street and the thirsty old dudes still trying to get a ride home with the young meat they found in the club.

"Uh, looks like you got got," He said. I walked around to the driver's side of the car and saw what he meant. A big yellow boot sitting on my wheel. Damn Park Atlanta. Why would they come through here Tonight of all nights? Well. I guess I'll have to just take care of this.

"Get in," I tell him.

"But you got booted. We could just…"

"Nah. Get in. I got it," I assure him. He shrugs again and bends down to fit in my car. I look around and kneel at the booted wheel. I look around again, just to make sure, and give the boot three solid taps with my first two fingers. There's a small crackling sound, and the boot falls off, clanging on the worn-down pavement. I smile and get up to push the boot out of my way. I get in the car and turn the ignition. He looks dumbfounded for a second but finds his voice again when I pull out of the space.

"Man, how did you do that?" he asks me.

I smile again and whip back onto Peachtree. "Let's just say I got a magic touch. We'll see if you have one too."

* * *

The sun came up on Friday morning and I came to my senses. Old dude was a waste, and I had class at 2. I kicked him out of my house and rushed to Clark around 10. I had just enough time to throw together a paper due that day in the library. It's not my best, but Ms. Perro will kill me if I try to turn in another late paper so it'll have to do. Lucky for me, because it's Friday the library is practically empty like the rest of campus. By 1:20, I have a finished paper ready to be printed out. Of course, the AUC library in all their wisdom decided that we need print cards to print out our work because, of course, they don't get enough money from us. So, I get up and walk to the printer, hoping that I still have money on my card.

No such luck.

"Come on, come on. All I need is three pages! Come on!" I yell to the printer.

"Shh!" Some chick says from behind me. "Some of us are trying to work!"

"Nobody's stopping you," I say back. I turn around to stare at her for a second and she stares back. She looks pissed; probably because she lives in this library. Glasses, a basic looking blue top and some faded jeans that probably were hand-me-downs from her mom. I'm not a fashion queen, but sis needs some help. She rolls her eyes and turns back to her screen, so I turn back to the printer. I try to swipe my print card again, but of course nothing happens. I take a deep breath to calm myself down. I know what I have to do, but I won't be able to do it if my mind isn't focused. I close my eyes and tap the printer three times. Just like last night, the air around the printer crackles and it whirs to life, spitting out the pages for my last-minute paper. I swear I love magic. I bend down to get the paper when I hear a voice behind me.

"How did you do that?" It's glasses girl from a minute ago.

"Huh? What?" I blurt out. I turn back around to face her and hope that I don't look too guilty.

"How. Did. You. Do. That." She repeats, pointing at the printer. "Your card wasn't working literally fifteen seconds ago." She has her print card in her hand, apparently, she had walked up to help me out and saw me magic the printer.

Shit.

"Oh, I had the funds on here, I just wasn't pressing the right buttons," I lie. No one has ever caught me doing magic before, so I don't know how to cover it up. "You know, it's been a few years since I've had to print out a paper in here so I forgot how it works."

She doesn't look too convinced. She narrows her eyes for a second and then smiles. "Oh yeah, I get it. Cool." She sticks her hand out for me to shake it. I take it; I'm just relieved she stopped asking questions. "I'm Amira Scott."

"Ja'Corey…" I say cautiously.

"Who's the paper for?"

"My English teacher, Ms. Perro." I answer. I'm still confused, but if she keeps asking about the work she won't ask about what I did to print it out. "She teaches at Clark."

"Oh, you're at Clark too? So am I! What classification?" She looks genuinely interested, so I keep answering her.

"Senior. Hopefully graduating," I tell her.

"Oh same. Clark really tries to keep you there for as long as they can. I'm getting out this time though. I'm gonna find a way or make one."

She smiles like her using the school's motto was the smartest, funniest thing in the world. Okay, time to cut this short.

"Well, thanks for trying to help, but I got it. See you around," I say. She stops me again.

"So how long have you known about your magic?" She pushes her glasses up on her face and blinks innocently a few times.

"My…what?" I'm in full blown panic mode now. How could she know…?

"Your magic, duh. That's how you got your paper to print. I used to do it all the time until my brother started guilting me for taking money out of the library's pocket. So now I have a print card like everyone else." She held up the print card as if it was the weirdest thing about this conversation. Meanwhile, I was shook. No one had ever seen me using magic, let alone had it themselves, if she even did. Here she was talking about magic-ing stuff like everybody could do it. I didn't know what to say.

"Oh…you didn't know other people had it did you?" Amira asks. "That's cool. I didn't know anyone but my brother until a few years ago. Oh! You should meet my brother! And hang out sometime!"

"Hold up," I say. "First of all, I don't know you like that. Second of all, you don't know what you're talking about. I don't have any 'magic'. Third of all, stay the hell away from me before I call public safety or a psychologist." I try to walk away from her and forget this conversation ever happened, but she reaches out to stop me. It just goes to show how empty this place is that there's no one around to catch all this.

"You're not the only one. There are others, if you wanna meet all of us. It will be fun!" Clearly this chick don't have friends.

"Yo, get off me and go get some help. You done watched too many Marvel movies."

Amira sighs and lets me go. For some stupid reason I don't take off running immediately. I guess I'm kind of intrigued after all. She reaches behind her and snatches a piece of paper out of her notebook. She taps it with her finger and says, "Address". I raise my eyebrows and almost immediately jump backwards when writing appears on the paper.

"What the hell?" I say.

"This is my address. I'll be at the house by 4 today. You should come by. You'll probably learn some stuff you never knew." She hands me the magic-ed address and pushes her glasses up again. I look from her to the paper, half expecting it (or her) to disappear and I wake up in bed with the minute man again. Neither happens.

"Why are you-why are you doing this?" I manage to get out.

"Duh, Ja'Corey. Us magical negroes gotta stick together," she says and sits back at her computer.

* * *

I spend all of Ms. Perro's class thinking about that weird talk with Amira. I was so distracted she tells me (for the hundredth time) that unless I don't wanna graduate in the spring (again) I better tighten up. Anyway, after class I head to my car and think. I look at the paper that Amira gave me. Maybe I should go check it out. Clearly, she knows about magic and she's right: I haven't met anyone else like me. I put the address Amira gave me in my GPS. They stay in the condos in Belmonte Hills. Well, at least it isn't far.

"Alright Maxine," I say to my car. "Let's go learn about some magic."

About ten minutes later, I pull into Belmonte Hills and rev the gas to get Maxine to the top of a hill in the complex. I look around for building 109 and park in front of it. I can see a few flowers growing in front of the tan condo and ignore the voice in my head telling me this is a bad idea long enough to knock on the door. I hear some shuffling around and a minute later the door opens and Amira is standing in it. I see her eyes light up behind her glasses when she recognizes me.

"Hi Ja'Corey! I hoped you would come!"

"You can just say 'Corey," I tell her.

"Okay 'Corey! Well, come on in!" She steps to the side and I scoot by her into the foyer. I can tell that this is a nice little place. I see two sets of stairs, one leading up and one leading down, and a big living room and dining room all decorated with nice furniture, paintings of Black people, and books. I shouldn't be surprised at the books. She's clearly a big nerd. The whole place looks decent though, if it didn't have this ugly brown carpet I might think about living here instead of the dorms. Amira leads me to the living room where some fine ass brown skinned dude is sitting on the couch watching TV. He looks up at me and I look at him. We lock eyes for a second before he looks away. He's gay.

"'Dre, this is 'Corey. The one I told you about," Amira says to him. He nods, never taking his eyes off the TV screen. I can see the lights from the screen reflecting off his glasses. Maybe it's because he's fine but he makes the glasses work a lot better than Amira. "This is De'Andre, my twin brother," Amira explains.

"'Sup," I say to him. He looks at me again. The more I look at him the more I can see that he and Amira are twins. Same "I'm smarter than you" expression, same rich brown skin tone, and the same hand me down looking clothes: in his case a red t-shirt and some khaki joggers.

"Hey," he says. Deep voice. I wonder if he's one of those that try to be more masculine than they are. Guess I'll find out.

I turn back to Amira. "Okay so you got me here. Now what? Are you gonna make me do some blood ritual? We gonna summon the Power of Three?"

Amira laughs. “No no! I just thought you would want to meet other trix.”

“‘Trix’?” I repeat. “Is that what you call yourselves?” I can’t help but think about how horrible a name that is.

“That’s what Amira calls us,” De’Andre clarified, still not moving from in front of the TV.

“Yes! It’s inconspicuous, not like calling us witches or anything. And it’s smart!” She looks at me, waiting on her brilliance to reach my mortal mind. It doesn’t, so she keeps going. “Trix, you know, after tricksters? Like what we have to be over her in America?” I only partway get it so I shrug. She sighs. “Most folks don’t get it, even here in this super Black school. It’s a shame really how few people know about our heritage,” she says sadly.

“You didn’t have many friends growing up, did you?” I ask her. De’Andre turns from the screen to glare at me, and Amira looks a little hurt. “Sorry, it was a joke,” I fumble. “So long as you stop calling me a magical negro I’m good with whatever.” I laugh a little to try to make her feel better. She smiles, so I guess it worked.

“Come sit down! I’m sure you have plenty of questions,” Amira says, leading me to the couch beside the loveseat De’Andre’s on. “It’s been a while since I’ve been able to meet another new trix.”

“If you’re giving a history lesson I’m going in the other room. I’m sure there’s something else I could be doing,” De’Andre announces. He pushes his glasses up and gets up from the couch to walk into the dining room. I watch him walk out of the room, and all the irritation I had with him is gone. He has a nice ass at least, even if he seems like an asshole. Maybe I'll get to…

"Don't mind him," Amira says, interrupting my thoughts. "He tries to pretend like he's not a trix, like he didn't use magic to get through a lot of his Morehouse classes."

"I didn't," De'Andre says. "I graduated on my own and got my job on my own too." He puts on some headphones and starts flipping pages in a book he got off the shelf. I squint to see the title. *Perfect Peace* by Daniel Black. I've heard about that book. It's supposed to be about this boy who gets raised as a girl and then back as a boy. If he's reading that he's definitely gay.

"Anyway!" Amira smiles at me. "So how long have you known about your magic?"

I shrug. "Since I was little I guess. I used to do stuff on accident. Get candy when I wasn't supposed to, get toys my parents didn't want me to have, you know. Kid stuff. It wasn't until high school that I really realized what it meant to have powers. Then I started doing some real magic stuff," I explain, remembering how many times magic helped me back then. "I probably wouldn't have graduated if I didn't have that extra help with papers and stuff."

"So, is that all you used your powers for? Nothing bigger?" Amira asks. "That's kids' stuff. I did that when I was in elementary," she jokes.

I hate being outdone. "Ummmm…I tried to get a date with them one time, but it didn't work."

"Oh, no wonder. It's really hard to use your magic on people unless you use 'chantments."

"Use what?" I ask. "You're letting your Atlanta come out."

"I'm not from Atlanta; we're from Arkansas," Amira corrects me.

"Still country," I point out. "What's a 'chantment?"

"A spell, basically," Amira clarifies. "Our grandma used to call them that when she was teaching us how to use our powers, so it just stuck."

"Your grandma was a…trix too?" I ask.

Amira nods. "Yep. She taught us everything there is to know about magic; the history, how it works, everything. Does anyone else in your family have magic?"

I shake my head. "They say my uncle was a little strange, but I don't know if he had magic." I admit that I was intrigued now. Apparently, the Scotts come from a long line of trix, and Amira was a historian of them. If she really was using her powers for bigger stuff, maybe should could teach me too. "So how do you use a-what you call it? A 'chantment?"

"I'll be glad to explain it to you! But first, do you know where our powers come from?" Amira asks. I shrug, so she continues. "You take any African American History courses over at Clark?" I nod. "Then you know about conjuring, right?" I nod again. "Our powers are stemmed from that. My great-great grandmother was a conjure woman; she and a bunch of people on the plantation with her refused to let their enslavers take away their culture. But they couldn't openly practice so they hid it as best they could and continued to teach it to their kids so the practice would never be lost."

"So, our powers are voodoo?" I interrupt. De'Andre laughs.

"No," Amira shakes her head. "First off, it would be Vudun, not that Hollywood stuff. Second of all, that's not the only type of magic Black people have. For our family, our powers come from conjuring. It's had to adapt and change over the years because what they need them for has changed. Whether it's hoodoo, conjuring, or any other belief, we as Black people have been slyly shaping the world for a long time. Our powers are just the newest version of that," she explains.

"Lemme guess, you're a History major?" I ask.

She smiles. "That, and I've taken a few classes in the African American Studies department. Dr. Black is great, and he inspired me to go read more."

I look around her at De'Andre still reading Dr. Black's book. I wonder if he inspires him too.

"Anyway," Amira says. I look back at her in time to catch her serious expression and her pushing up her glasses again. "I think your family had to have come from one of those people with Great-Great Grandma Sara. If I'm right, you should be able to cast 'chantments and everything else, just like us."

I let her words sink in for a moment. It seemed right somehow. For as long as I had been using my powers, I had wanted more. To know more, to do more, to use them more. It seemed like Amira had that for me.

"So, can you teach me how to use a 'chantment? Like, how does it work?"

"I'm glad you asked!" Amira grins. She gets up from the couch and walks in the dining room to De'Andre.

"No to whatever it is," De'Andre says.

"I don't need you anyway," Amira says back. She grabs a candle from the kitchen and comes back to the couch. "It's all about intent and language. You have to believe what you're doing and know how to ask for it to happen. When you know what you want, you can call it however you want. Watch this."

She holds the candle away from her face so we both can see it well, and she says one word: "Lit." Suddenly, the candle lights, and I can't help but jump backwards. Both De'Andre and Amira laugh at me.

"How did you do that?" I ask.

"Weren't you listening? Intent and knowing how to ask for what you want. You have to believe that what you want to happen can happen, and you have to have the language to call for it."

"But 'lit' is like, slang or whatever. That's not an African language, or African anything," I tell her. Everything I've heard about knowing words and language in my classes referred back to Africa in some way.

Amira grins at me. I can tell she is enjoying being my teacher. "It is African; Black folks made the word! We've been changing language and using it for what we want to use it for for years. Good luck finding anything that's popular now that Black folks didn't come up with, words or otherwise. Now watch this: "Litty," she says, and suddenly the whole room lights up like there are a hundred candles shining all over the living room. I have to cover my eyes because it's so bright. Amira waves her hand and says, "Black AF," and the lights on the candle and in the room dim. "See? You have to know what to say otherwise you'll never get anything done."

"Okay, that was cool," I admit. "Can you teach me how to do that?"

"Yeah, of course! That's why I wanted—"

"It's gonna have to wait," De'Andre interrupts. "Tayveon just text me and said he was heading up to Lenox to pick up Mikayla and wanted to know if we wanted to meet him there before he goes to work."

"Oh. Okay. Tell him yeah." She turns back to me and asks me if I want to meet some more trix. I look at De'Andre and he tries to avoid my gaze.

"Sure," I say, smiling at him.

* * *

When you've been here for a while, Lenox isn't really somewhere you go regularly. I moved here from Alabama five years ago, and I can probably count the times I've been here. It's a tourist trap; folks come here from around the country hoping to see some celebrities or pay ridiculous prices. I don't understand how people like Amira and De'Andre even get in their minds to come here, but apparently their friends Mikayla and Tayveon aren't like them. De'Andre called them "future Huxtables"; Amira said they were just from a different space. I read that as they're bougie as hell. Just what I need on a Friday. Stuck up Black people.

"Tayveon said they're already heading to the food court. He said he only has a little while before he goes in Tonight, so he needs to eat," De'Andre announces when we walk towards the food court. I look around at all the people ducking in and out of overpriced stores in their best outfits. These people really be coming in here tryna get chose.

"Okay cool. I was in the mood for some Chipotle anyway," Amira says. She walks up towards the restaurant, knowing that it will probably take them a little while longer to make her food. That leaves me with her fine ass mute of a brother.

"How can she eat that stuff? Doesn't she know that they shut a bunch of stores down for nasty food?" I ask.

De'Andre shrugs. "You use 'chantments like she does and you tend not to sweat the small stuff. Not when you can just speak the sickness away with an 'I'm good' or something." He walks ahead of me towards Five Guys, and I'm suddenly reminded of a Trillville line. I follow him to the line and we both order.

"Aye! 'Dre!" Some guy booms from behind us. De'Andre turns around and sees some bulky football player-looking dude flagging him down. He puts his tree trunk sized arm down and I get a better look at the loose white t-shirt that drapes over his mahogany skin and black Adidas track pants. He has to play some type of sport. Sitting in the chair beside him is a very embarrassed looking dark-skinned girl with her hair pulled back in a tight ponytail. She's wearing a pink Abercrombie and Fitch Polo and some tan slacks. She hits him on the shoulder before she tries to hide her face. So, they're dating and he's the embarrassing boyfriend. Figures. Bougie Black girls need an athlete I guess. She looks like she just got off work and he looks like he's relaxing before he goes in, so I assume this is Tayveon and Mikayla. De'Andre smiles and walks over to their table, so I follow. His smile is cute too. He need to stop playing.

"So, is this the new one?" Tayveon asks. "I'm Tayveon." He holds his hand out for me to shake it as I try to sit down. His hands are about as big as the napkin dispensers. I know he probably makes Mikayla very happy.

"Mikayla Andrews," Mikayla herself says. "And you are…?"

"Ja'Corey Washington," I say to both of them. Mikayla nods and smiles sweetly. She doesn't give off bougie. At least not yet.

"Where's Amira?" Tayveon asks.

"At Chipotle," De'Andre answers.

"That girl is going to die one day fooling with Chipotle," Mikayla says while shaking her head. I look at the big Chick-Fil-A salad in front of her, and I realize that she is definitely bougie.

"Couldn't she just, you know, say something like, 'Go Live' so she could not die?" I ask. De'Andre shakes his head, and Mikayla and Tayveon look at me for a second. I'm thinking I'm on to something when Mikayla answers my question.

"We couldn't do anything like that," she says calmly.

"Yeah. Everyone knows the 'chantment would be something like 'Turn Up!' or something like that," Tayveon adds.

"Really? It's that easy?" I was joking at first. All three of them bust out laughing and I join in.

"No! We aren't immortal. We can just make stuff happen." Tayveon explained. He reaches a huge arm over the table and pats me on my shoulder. His plate sized hand sends a shake through my whole body, but I don't let him see that. "You funny. I bet you get hella females." Mikayla rolls her eyes beside him.

"Um, take the f.e. off and you'll be right," I say with a laugh. I've never been shy about my sexuality, so I hope it won't be an issue for them either. I do a quick glance around the table to see their reactions. Mikayla shrugs and gets back to her salad, De'Andre looks at me some more but says nothing, and poor Tayveon takes a second to figure it out.

"Oh! Well, that's cool. Do you man," he says when it dawns on him. He tears back into whatever Philly cheese steak he ordered. Behind us, Amira finally walks up at the same time Five Guys calls De'Andre and I's orders.

"I'll get them," De'Andre offers. I nod and watch him walk away again. Mikayla snorts and I look at her. All she does is smile.

"So, I guess everyone got all acquainted?" Amira asks.

"Yes, we're all one big happy family now," Mikayla says. Tayveon laughs and puts his arm around her shoulder.

"Where'd Amira find you?" He asks me.

"You make it seem like I just go around recruiting trix!" Amira says back. De'Andre walks up and sets my food in front of me before sitting down with his own. I thank him.

"You do!" Mikayla and Tayveon say in unison. "She approached me in Georgia State's bookstore when I used to work there," Mikayla begins. "She saw me tap a shelf to straighten the books on it and bombarded me with questions."

"That's nothing. She saw me at a party one night doing a trick for some other guys on the team. She walked up and did my trick better than me! Then gone tell me, 'If I wanna do this right I gotta talk with her some more,' like I don't know how to use my own magic!" Tayveon complains.

"You didn't," Amira says simply. "None of you knew anything about 'chantments before we started hanging out."

"Yeah well now we do. I bet I could beat you in a spell off now!" Tayveon boasts.

"What's a spell off?" I ask, even though I'm pretty sure I have an idea.

"Basically, it's where two people cast 'chantments at each other until one gives. Nobody beats Amira because she knows all the 'chantments," Mikayla explains.

"I almost did one time!" Tayveon argues.

"I doubt that," I say before I can stop myself. De'Andre laughs. I might just have him yet.

"Oh yeah? I'd like to see you try! In fact, try something right now. Cast a 'chantment, let's see what she's taught you!" Tayveon says to me.

Before I can say something back to the big bear Amira interrupts. "We just met today; he hasn't even tried any 'chantments yet."

Mikayla and Tayveon looked shocked. "What? Do you even conjure, bro?" Tayveon asks.

"Look, I'm new. I've done stuff, just not like y'all have. I bet when I get some 'chantments down I'll be able to—" I stop talking because of the next words I hear being yelled across the food court.

"All these fuckin' faggots bruh!" Some dude yells from a few tables across from us. A femme dude has just walked by his table rocking a tight blouse, tight pants, laid hair, and a sick bag. "This why I hate Atlanta, for real bruh," he says to the other two guys sitting with him.

“That ain’t what you said last night,” the femme dude spits back. I admire his bravery, but that probably wasn’t the best move.

“What the fuck you say to me bitch?” The guy practically screams. He leaps up from the table with his other two friends. The femme dude keeps walking, and now all eyes are on the three homophobic assholes, including the eyes of the security guard.

“It ain’t worth it man,” one of the assholes say to the asshole-in-chief. He nods and they all sit back down. I breathe a sigh of relief that this didn’t get ugly, but that quickly turns to anger, especially when the security guard leaves.

“I hate homophobes,” is all I manage to get out through my gritted teeth.

“Well, allow me to help you feel better,” Mikayla offers. She looks directly at the table of them, particularly the leader. He lifts up his cup to drink from it, and she says in a clear voice, “Mask off.” The top of his cup flies off, and the dark colored liquid inside spills onto his good white t-shirt. He leaps up from the table in shock and anger while his boys laugh at him. We snicker a bit too.

“Good one, bae!” Tayveon cheers. “Let me add a little something.”

“Oh, can I join in?” Amira says excitedly.

“Sure can,” Tayveon grins. They both turn to look at the table where the two followers are still laughing at their leader's attempts to clean his shirt. "Tied down," Tayveon says.

"Hit it," Amira adds. The head homophobe tries to walk forward back to his seat, but he trips like his shoelaces were tied together. He falls forward onto the table and hits it, which somehow causes the other two assholes food to fall on their laps, ruining all of their clothes. They all start cursing at each other, and all five of us fall out laughing.

"What's so fuckin' funny?" The idiot leader yells over at us.

"You," I say and keep laughing.

"What you say?!" He barks at me. He starts pushing tables out the way to try to get to us.

"Now's your chance, try a 'chantment!" Amira whispers. I agree with her, it would be fun to add to the humiliation. Only problem is, I can't think of anything to say. I can tell that the words are all like slang or sayings, but what would correspond with me doing something to him? And what do I want to do to him? Things were so much easier when all I had to do was tap stuff to make it do what I wanted.

I look up and the dude is almost at our table, looking mad as ever. By now more people in the food court are watching to see if there's gonna be a good old-fashioned fight. It may have to be if I can't think of anything to magic him with.

"Drop them draws," I hear De'Andre say, and sure enough as he was walking the bully's pants hit the ground. Lucky for him, De'Andre lets him keep on his actual draws, but we all see enough to know why he probably is so angry at everyone. The guy stops in the middle of the food court and falls over again, this time with his (decent looking) ass face up into the sky. Everybody who can see him laughs, and old boy has to be dumb embarrassed now. He picks up his pants and hobbles off into the nearest store, leaving his boys messy and angry at their table and all of us in tears.

After we all collect ourselves, Tayveon looks at me. "Well, I can't pretend like I got 'chantments the first day either—"

"Try the first week," Amira adds.

"Anyway! You got time little bruh. Today was fun though."

"Sure was," Mikayla agreed. "And you even got to see De'Andre use his magic. That's a rare sight."

"I bet it is," I agree and look over at De'Andre. "Thank you, by the way."

"You're welcome," he says, never looking up from his burger. "Just don't get used to it."

"Oh, I'm sure I could get used to it. There are a few things I could definitely get used to," I say back. He looks up at me and we lock eyes again. He can't help but smile a little bit as he looks away again.

"Well I could definitely get used to this!" Amira interjects. "Five trix just hanging out, casting 'chantments and protecting the innocent!"

"So now we're superheroes?" De'Andre asks.

"No! I mean, but we could be! Think about it: going all over Atlanta, helping people with their problems and righting wrongs. We could do it!"

"That sounds too much like magical negroes," I tell her. Mikayla and De'Andre laugh.

"What's a magical negro?" Tayveon asks.

"Surely not you man," I tell him with a smile. I tap De'Andre under the table and we both laugh as Tayveon sits there even more confused. De'Andre looks at me once more, and this time we keep glance. He smiles that pretty smile and goes back to his burger. I got him. No 'chantments needed.

The Messiah Curse

By

Gerald L. Coleman

The dream was always the same. It began with the impertinence of a rising street covered in uneven, cobbled stone, followed by the intemperance of its aimless winding as it passed between two and three-story houses, which were huddled together as if they were seeking comfort from one another. A vibrant throng of angry voices emanated from the mob lining the street. Every texture of human emotion was in the air as the mob surged and receded around a stooped figure like water as the tide was coming in. Antipathy resounded above all the others. The hostility was so palpable, he could taste it. It was all shoving, and fists in the air, mixed with curses and spiting. What did anger taste like? Burnt toast? Sour milk?

He was weak – a shadow of a man, easily swayed by the will of others. So, he joined in. The air was hot with the smell of cheap wine. The stale odor of old sweat mixed with fear. What does fear smell like? The coppery scent of blood? A sharp, twinge of lemon peel in the nose? It was clear, upon hindsight, that the thick cloud of hostility had been borne of fear, not anger. It had not been remotely justified. But, human beings feared what they did not understand and despised even more those who held up a mirror to their ugliness. Out of it all, though, those penetrating brown eyes haunted him the most. They pierced him to his core, like a hot knife inserted between his ribs and plunged into his heart. He felt naked. Not the kind where one's clothes sat in a haphazard bundle on the floor. No, it was the kind of naked, where all your secrets are laid bare. The taunts he was shouting suddenly caught in his throat. And then, the beleaguered man spoke.

Azriel jerked upright in bed, flinging his blanket off in a confusion of pillows and sheets as he reached for something that wasn't there. It took him a moment to realize that it was just a dream. No matter how many times it happened, he could never remember that it was a dream. It was as if he had fallen through time and landed in his bed. His heart raced in his chest. Sweat clung to him like an oil slick on the ocean's surface. *Breathe*, he told himself. *Just breathe.* The dream never changed. The moment hunted him, while he slept, like a hungry wolf in a familiar forest he could not escape. He slid to the edge of the bed, dangled his legs over the edge, and placed his feet on the thick, white rug below them. In, hold, and out – was how he breathed for the next few minutes until his heart rate slowed. He reached over to the white nightstand, grabbed his cell phone, and touched the screen. When it glowed to soft-white life, he was able to see the number five glaring back at him. It was way too early, but there was never any going back to sleep after the dream. He rubbed his hands over his face and decided to get up.

Azriel crossed the bedroom to the bathroom and turned on the shower. White striations swirled through the gray tile behind the full-length, glass door. Shower jets were imbedded in the ceiling and walls creating a cross-stream of spraying water. He set it to a heavy mist before stepping in. When he had the place remodeled, an instant water heater was installed, so there was no need to wait. He placed his hands on the wall and let the steaming water wash the last echoes of the dream away along with the night sweat. He wasn't sure how long he stood there, but, finally, he reached for soap and a wash cloth.

After cleaning up, Azriel threw on a white tee and blue, striped, pajama pants. He changed the sheets and made his bed before heading downstairs. As he drifted down the stairs, he slid his hand across a clean-shaven head and jaw. He shaved at night, before bed, so his mornings were less pre-occupied with personal grooming. The kitchen-dining-living room was a single, large, open area demarcated by how the furniture was arranged. The kitchen and dining area were separated by a long, wide, island with a white marble top, streaked through with gray lines. The marble sat on a stainless-steel body filled with drawers. The rest of the kitchen matched the aesthetic of the island – *modern chic.*

By the time Azriel began fixing breakfast the sun was creeping through the floor-to-ceiling windows lining the right wall. The golden light created a soft, warm glow in the living room. He cut a thick piece of crusty ciabatta bread, sliced an avocado, and added two eggs over medium to the rectangular plate with rounded edges. He sprinkled the eggs with a shaved parmesan that was aged for ten years, a bit of extra-virgin olive oil, and a dash of salt and pepper.

The most expensive thing in his kitchen was his espresso machine. It had a double boiler, rotary pump, digital thermostat, pressure gauges, spring-loaded steam and water valves, as well as insulated steam and hot water wands. It was a work of art shape from stainless steel. But, even the best espresso machine is an utter waste without a machine capable of grinding espresso beans properly. His sat on the white, marble counter beside the espresso machine, right between the sink and the stainless-steel refrigerator. The grinder cost nearly as much as the espresso machine. He ground his fresh, roasted beans with the sound of spinning burrs churning inside the grinder. Next, he tamped the grounds down in the shining basket of the portafilter, before twisting the portafilter into place inside the ring of the head of the espresso machine.

It was an involved ritual. Grabbing the stainless- steel pitcher, which had been sitting in the refrigerator to keep it cold, he turned on the pump on the espresso machine until a thin stream of whistling steam came racing out of the long, thin steel steam arm. Soon, he had worked the steam into the milk until he had a thick micro-foam. Azriel lifted the lever that started the brew-cycle and watched as the thin, creamy lines of dark-brown espresso poured out into the waiting cup below. Mixing the espresso with the sugar he spooned into the cup, he poured in the micro-foam mixed with steamed milk until the cup was full. With his coffee made, he placed the cup on its saucer, grabbed his plate, and walked over to the dining table.

Sometimes he ate with the television on, but, he'd recently stopped watching the news. The Americans had elected a buffoon as their new chief executive and he did not care to watch the circus. While it wasn't the first time he'd witnessed someone utterly unqualified being given authority, this time seemed more egregious than most. This morning, like most mornings following the dream, he ate with soft music playing in the background. Tapping a few virtual buttons on his cellphone, he elicited sounds from the wireless speakers installed throughout his home. As Marvin Gaye crooned, *I come up hard baby, but now I'm cool*, and *Trouble Man* echoed through the room, Azriel focused his attention on how crusty the thick bread was, and how the rich olive oil mixed with bits of shaved parmesan complimented the buttery flavor of the avocado slices mingling with the soft-cooked egg. He washed it all down with the caramelly-sweet intoxication of the espresso mixed with foamy, steamed milk. Slowly, the haunting memory of his recurring nightmare faded, even as the glow of the early morning sunlight flooded in brightening everything around him. By the time he was staring at the bottom of his empty cup, coated with the last dregs of brown espresso crema and white, milk foam, he was ready to get dressed and start the day in earnest.

Just like traveling over land was so much faster – you could go from one side of the world to the other in hours rather than months – coffee tasted better, and dentistry was exponentially superior, clothes were also made better. It was somewhere between late fall and early winter in Atlanta. The air was cool, though not yet cold. Even though it was Saturday, he still had a meeting. Azriel went back upstairs and slipped into black, fitted jeans, a black polo, and black, dress boots. He slid a black, leather belt with a small silver buckle, through his pant loops and the leather loops of a black holster tucked into his pants, just behind his right hip. Then, he grabbed his *Sacramentals*.

The first one lay in an antique, Persian box sitting on his white dresser. It had been called a *Gentleman's Box* when he first began using it to store his weapon. The box was brown wood with middle-eastern inlay in mother of pearl and Syrian marquetry. It was covered in geometric designs of Moorish origins. It was a work of art and nearly two-hundred years old. Azriel smiled as he ran his hand over its carved surface. He lifted the lid and pulled out the modified Wilson Combat 1911 laying on a padded bed of purple silk. The scrollwork running along the slide and down the frame was in a language no longer spoken by men. Finding the materials for the ceremony that would change it from a simple firearm to a metaphysical weapon had been difficult. Locating a mystic for the ceremony was an even more arduous proposition, but ultimately worth it. Though, he would not be going back to the Sahara anytime soon.

For some reason, he was crazy enough to follow a Benin Voodoo Priestess into the *Eye of Africa*, deep in the heart of the Sahara, at midnight. It was something he would never forget. While golden grains of sand howled around him like a whirlwind, Azriel was comforted by the fact that he had seen things that would turn a hardened soldier's hair white. But what that woman did, standing in the middle of the blue spiral known as the *Richat Structure* by astronauts who could see the formation from space, changed his understanding of darkness. When she was done, she handed the black gun back to him, with smoke rising off it, covered in ancient runes, which looked like decorative embellishments if you didn't look too closely. According to her, the kind of bullets no longer mattered. Where he had once relied on blessed bullets that had been conjured over, he could now fire any ammunition that was the right caliber for the gun, and it would do the job.

Holding it in his right hand, he pressed the release, ejecting the magazine into his left. He checked to see that it was full of the .45 ACP tactical rounds he preferred, before sliding it back in place with a solid *click*. The barrel made a nearly identical sound when he pulled it back and released it, feeding a round into the chamber. With it loaded, he thumbed the safety on, and tucked the gun into the holster strapped on at five o'clock, just behind his right hip. Behind his left hip, at eight o'clock, he snapped on two, black, leather, magazine pouches and slid a seven-round magazine into each.

After lowering the lid on the box, he reflexively checked to make sure the small, gold, Akkadian medallion still hung around his neck. It was inscribed with the eight-pointed star of Anunnaki. Assured that it was still hanging there, he opened the second box sitting on his dresser and pulled out a black, Rolex submariner, along with the large, gold ring sitting next to it. The ring was engraved with the Eye of Heru, bound between a falcon and a serpent. He slipped it on his left-hand ring finger before securing the watch on his left wrist. Assured in the comfort provided by the Sacramentals being on his person, Azriel threw on his leather jacket, grabbed his cellphone and wallet, and made his way downstairs. Once he hit the main floor, he walked through the living room over to the door in the far wall. He pulled open the door to the garage and stepped through it.

During the renovation, he decided to keep the delivery bay of the business that was once located on the lot in order to turn it into a garage. Closing the door behind, to what was once an office, he strolled past his weights, benches, treadmill, and heavy bag to where his car was parked. Azriel glanced over at his café racer, but then decided to take the car. There was a chance of rain later in the day. Riding a motorcycle in the rain was not his idea of a pleasant experience.

A turn of the key and the seven-hundred horsepower, Edelbrock-supercharged, Coyote crate engine in his nineteen sixty-six mustang Fastback roared to life. The car was rebuilt by a small outfit in Wisconsin, which specialized in customized restoration. It was a thing of beauty. The stance was lower and more aggressive than its stock alternative. The paint scheme was a unique blue-gray for the body with a black hood, roof, and grill. Bits of red adorned it, here and there, as a highlight. Large wheels with satin-black rims, red brake calipers, and matching red rotors, finished the look. Azriel clicked the garage opener hanging on the visor and revved the engine while the door slowly rose. The garage opened onto the back of his home. Once he pulled out, he clicked the opener so the garage door closed behind him. By the time it had, he was already turning onto Atlanta road. The area was a semi-warehouse district halfway between downtown Atlanta and Vinings.

There were two reasons he chose to renovate a property in the area rather than buying something already finished. It was sparsely populated and only subject to traffic for a brief span in the late afternoon. The rest of the time it was fairly private and out of the way. He liked his privacy. It was also safer for other people for him to live in a less populated area. Driving down Atlanta road, he passed the headquarters for the Atlanta Ballet on his left. There was also a Pepsi bottling facility, several nondescript small businesses, two trucking companies, and a strip club. Had he turned left onto Atlanta road instead of right, he would have passed a defunct gas station turned mini-mart, a couple of self-storage companies, and a cemetery on the corner. He crossed a small bridge before turning left onto Marietta. The small, winding backroad took him to his destination.

As he drove down Marietta Road's small hill, he could see the spires of downtown Atlanta in the distance. To his immediate left, stood new luxury apartments. They were well-located but overpriced – though he would not have minded being able to leave his home, cross one street, and walk into a coffee shop, or any of the several restaurants in the immediate vicinity. The area was very much like Midtown but without the hassle. Azriel parked on the street, exited his car, and stepped onto the sidewalk. The air carried a hint of winter. Today was the first day of fall where the temperature dropped into the low sixties. He didn't mind. In fact, Azriel enjoyed being able to wear jackets, coats, and sweaters. Colorful leaves crunched under his boot as he strolled into the tiny parking lot that fronted Octane Coffee Bar.

He passed the small, bespoke, men's shop next door, called Thomas Wages, and stepped through the propped-open door to the coffee shop's interior.

The coffee bar layout opened up to the right of the door, but Azriel continued walking straight ahead. Entering the short hallway to the left of the register, he stepped past the two bathrooms on his right, and walked toward the blank wall dead ahead. To mortals that's exactly what it was – a blank wall. But, to Azriel, or any of the others like him, it was much more. There were many names for those who would be able to see a door that remained invisible to mortals. They were called the Fallen, the Fairie, Extramundane, Fae, or even Immortals – though many were not, in fact, immortal. Some knew them as Shadowwalkers, or the Undying – even, the Cursed. Many, over the centuries, had simply called them monsters. Most of the names were reductive or insufficient to describe everything, or everyone, that lurked in the shadows, filled the books of lore, haunted the dreams of men, or went bump in the night. The only one Azriel ever got comfortable being called was the *Long-lived.*

There it stood, at the end of the small hallway nearly everyone saw as the way to the restrooms. The door was simple wood, but painted red, with a gold sigil in the shape of the sign for infinity. They all looked the same. Azriel turned the golden knob, pulled the door open, and entered. As he was closing it behind him, a young woman turned into the hallway, presumably heading for a bathroom. Her face went from startled to alarmed as it dawned on her that she had never seen the door Azriel was walking through. He smiled at her and closed it behind him. He knew what would happen next. The giant, red ruby, embedded over the door, would fill the hallway with a flash of light invisible to the naked eye. He did not have to open the door again to know that the door, and the sight of him holding it open, had been erased from the woman's memory. At that very moment, she was likely standing in the hallway wondering why was there before suddenly remembering she was on her way to the bathroom.

Azriel made his way down the hidden stairwell behind the red door. Three flights down and he was walking into a very different bar, but one with the same name. It had become easier, over time, to simply call the *Hidden Places* by the same names as their fronts. The Octane was his favorite haunt. Like the one above it, it served coffee, other drinks, and food. It also served more exotic forms of nourishment meant for the various kinds of beings who lived in the *Otherworld* – the one that existed behind the world of mortals – the one right in front of them, which they could not see. The other difference between this Octane, and the one above, meant for mortals, was a much more luxurious décor. Instead of small café tables that wobbled, and hard, wooden chairs, there were wide booths with oversized, leather couches, heavy, wood tables with large, plush armchairs, and discreet sections hidden behind diaphanous curtains. The floor was covered in a lush, blood-red carpet. The lighting was warm, but dim. And, there was a long bar with red, leather sides and a black, marble top.

It was early, so it was no surprise that there was no one else in the main room. Azriel was early for his meeting, so he grabbed his favorite table on the far side of the cafe. It put his back against the wall and gave him clear sight lines of the entire bar. Epiphanus approached the table with a double espresso. Azriel smiled and nodded at the tall, thin man. He was pale, pleasant, but quiet. He wore blue velvet pants, and a powder-blue shirt with Italian cuffs. A quick glance down revealed brown, wingtip brogues, with a two-tone, brown patina stain. A white hand towel hung neatly folded over his forearm. His voice was much deeper than might have been expected.

He rumbled, “Good morning, Wanderer. I made your usual doppio. Can I get you anything else?”

Azriel replied, “Good morning, Ep. The chessboard?”

With a smirk, Epiphanus sat the cup and saucer down in front of Azriel. He returned to the bar and retrieved a chessboard with a game in progress. It was beautifully-carved wood in silver, brown, and gray. The spaces alternated between heavily-carved blue, gray, and brown squares and plain, brown ones. The pieces were light-gray and brown on one side and tan and gray on the other. Their weighted wood was sculpted to match the board. All in all, it was a lovely board, though it was nothing like the cast-iron antique set he had at home. His was one of five sets made in Germany in 1850 by the master craftsman Gerhardt Klausman, shortly after the failed 1848 March Revolution, and just as Prussia was entering the industrial revolution before Bismarck achieved unification in 1871. The Klausman had tall, slender, delicately rendered pieces that were fashioned from heavy, cast-iron – an anachronism the artisan had prided himself on. The man was a genius with his hands and was gifted with a high tolerance for dark, German beer. The pieces matched the chest table they came with. Also made of heavy iron, the top was round, with the square board inset – both heavily engraved with scroll-work in brown, gray, burgundy, and gold. Azriel had spent countless hours sitting at that table working on his game.

The chessboard showed the standing match between Azriel and Epiphanus. They were a full year in. Today, it was his turn to move. Epiphanus thought he was going to put Azriel in check in twelve moves, and mate shortly thereafter. But, Azriel was running a long con on him. The man thought he was on the verge of victory. Only, when Azriel finally *castled,* it would become clear to Epiphanus that he was on the verge of losing – in three moves. As Epiphanus carefully sat the chessboard down on the table in front of him, with no attempt to hide a smug grin, Azriel schooled his own features. He narrowed his eyes, while pressing his lips firmly together as though troubled by what the board was showing him.

In the next hour, he sipped espresso, made it look like he was trying out different moves in his head, and waited for his meeting. Soon enough, Hopscotch McGavin slid into the chair across from him like a slimy snake slithering through high grass. There were few men Azriel knew as odd, or shifty, as Hopscotch. He put the shade in shady. The scrawny man earned the nickname Hopscotch by always being on the move from one place to the next – and always being willing to jump sides at the first sign of trouble, or after being paid to do so. Dirty-blonde hair fell into his blue eyes as he scratched at his thick beard. The suit was an expensive British label in jort-blue with a soft sheen. The jacket was cut high at the waist with a single button, peak lapels, and a single vent up the back. The black shirt looked like Italian silk patterned with blue, silver, white, and red flowers. It had a wide, spread collar, French cuffs without cufflinks, and was buttoned to the neck without a tie. He was also wearing black, double monk strap, leather boots. A white-gold, diamond encrusted, Audemars Piguet Chronograph hung loosely on his wrist, like it was still the nineties. For all of that, he smelled like cheap cologne.

Hopscotch smiled lazily at Azriel and ordered a drink; it was Grey Goose on the rocks. The smell told him that the man was more than a few drinks into the day. Azriel put up with Hopscotch because the man could get just about anything you wanted for the right price. You just had to remember never to turn your back on him, especially when money was changing hands.

Sliding the chess set over, out of the way, he said, "Hello, Hopscotch. I'm glad you could make it. You look like you're in the middle of something. Are you in the middle of something, Hop?"

Hopscotch unbuttoned his jacket, shaking his head a little too much, as his drink arrived. He downed it in one swallow, waving his free hand erratically, and said, "No, no, no. Not at all, Wanderer. Everything is copasetic."

Azriel tried not to roll his eyes. Hopscotch liked slang that was way past its use-by date. He thought it made him sound hip – *retrograde*, he called it, as if it was a fashion forward movement, or avant-garde. The man grinned widely, leaned back in his chair, and continued, "Azriel Stone. So, how are you, my guy? Looking good as usual. You still driving that pristine-ass Mustang? I keep telling you I can get you a hundred thou' easy, maybe more?"

Azriel shook his head, "How many times do I have to tell you, Hop. The car is not for sale. Now, do you have what I asked you for?"

The slender man leaned forward, reached inside his suit jacket to the small of his back, and produced a sheathed knife. He laid it on the table and said, "Tah. Dah. Motherfucker." Then he smiled, indicating the knife with both hands, like an infomercial salesman. It was a Persian Caucasian qama, also known as a double-edged dagger, from the 18th century. It had a broad, straight blade that was embellished with lotus palmettes, scrolling lines, and golden clouds giving the steel a black sheen. The hilt and wood scabbard were covered in similar ornamentations. It once belonged to a powerful Mazdayasna Magi who fought a dozen Shades at the ruins of the Zoroastrian temple of *Pir-e-Narak* near Yazd, and lived to tell about it. The dagger had been old even then. Azriel heard whispers about it for years but felt no need to seek it out until he lost his last dagger fighting a Shadowwalker in Seville, Spain the month before. He needed a replacement so he put Hopscotch on the trail of it. The man had actually produced.

Azriel said, "How much, Hop."

Hopscotch pulled his chair closer, wet his lips, leaned over the table, and was about to launch into his sales pitch when Azriel held up his hand and interrupted. "No." Shaking his head, he continued, "No, Hop, don't even try it. Listen to me. You have one shot to make this deal. I'm not going to haggle with you. I have two other feelers out on similar artifacts, so I don't have to have this one. Here's what we're going to do. You're going to give me a number – one number. And I'll either pay it, or I'll get up, leave, and buy one of the other artifacts that I have no doubt are on the way. I suggest you make it a good number."

Hopscotch clamped his mouth shut, swallowing whatever bullshit he had been about to spit. Narrowing his eyes, he stared at Azriel, no doubt trying to ascertain whether he was bluffing. After a moment, he swallowed hard again, waved his hands over the table like a magician doing a reveal or a maid indicating the table was clean, and said, "Thirty thousand."

Azriel looked at the dagger sitting on the table again. He stared at it for a moment, looked back up at Hopscotch, and said, "Sold."

He reached into his leather jacket, pulled out an orange envelope, and removed three stacks of bills. Sliding the envelope back into his jacket pocket, he pushed the money over to Hopscotch and grabbed the dagger.

"Nice doing business with you, Hop. You take care of yourself."

Without waiting to hear the man's response, Azriel headed for the door. As he passed the bar, he slid Epiphanus a ten for the espresso. The man flashed him a salute with two fingers before he went back to wiping off the bar. Soon, Azriel was back on the street headed for his car. His stomach growled when he reached the driver's side door, so he decided to head over to Café Intermezzo in Midtown for lunch.

The sun was up, and the weather was still right between warm and cool, but it was pleasant. Atlanta was alive with its usual bustling ambivalence. Thankfully, Café Intermezzo was only ten minutes away without the need to get on a highway or interstate. It was Saturday, so he could avoid the normal downtown traffic. He pulled out onto Marietta, made a left onto Northside, and a right onto 10th. When he reached Peachtree, eight minutes later, he turned left. One block up and he was parking.

Café Intermezzo was once located further down Peachtree toward Lenox Mall. Azriel had enjoyed that location. In his mind, it had more character. Now, the quaint bistro's new location was a bright, glitzy spot with a lovely patio, tucked into the base of one of the many nondescript buildings closer to the center of Midtown. He still missed the old place, with its dark corners, high tables, and a bar that looked like something out of the nineteen-twenties. Nevertheless, the food was still delicious. He sat in the main room by the wall of windows and ordered a Caesar salad, Viennese Salmon, and a decadently-sweet piece of cheese cake covered in mixed-berries and offset with a swirling dollop of whip cream on top. It left him satiated in the best way.

The rest of the day was all errands. He stopped at his UPS post office box to retrieve some mail and a few packages, including some new cigars and roasted espresso beans. He did not receive mail at home. Its location in a commercial district, along with not receiving mail there, was part of keeping his whereabouts hidden. After leaving the UPS store in Midtown, he stopped in Channing Valley at Sid Mashburn. A text had informed him that the hand-tailored suits he ordered were ready. While he was there he grabbed a pair of green foliage, diadora sneakers, which looked a bit like a pair of seventies-era Nike Cortez. It was on his way back to the car that he noticed the black Mercedes. Putting the three suit bags and the sneakers in his trunk, Azriel tried to remember if he had seen the car earlier. Sid Mashburn was located in a kind of warehouse-style building on the second floor. Its blue walls and dark gray awnings stood out against the painted, white, brick walls of the rest of the building. The parking area fronted the entire lot. And though there were other specialty shops in the complex, it was situated in such a way that it was difficult to be inconspicuous. With no other parking available, they had chosen to park in the far-left corner near the street. The tinted windows, the running engine, and the fact that they never got out of the car were all warning signs that set off his senses.

Azriel did not let on. He simply got in his car and pulled off. The sun was going down, so he turned onto Marietta NW and drove the two miles to Five Points. A left on Peachtree, a right on Ellis, took him to Freedom Parkway and Ponce De Leon. Barnett took him to Virginia and he pulled over to park beneath the trees, a few hundred yards from the corner of Virginia and Highland. Sure enough, the black Mercedes cruised by, rolling through the light in order to park further down on Virginia. Azriel got out and made like he was walking to Murphy's for dinner. But then, he turned onto North Highland. By the time the sun was down, he was walking around the right side of a small, local coffee shop called Press and Grind. It had a small, three-car lot in the front. Azriel walked through it and down the sloped drive on the right side of the building. He walked to the back and waited in the shadows. It was dark, quiet, and out of the line of sight to the sidewalk. It was perfect.

Three, large men in dark suits came lumbering around the corner. When Azriel was sure they were also out of the direct line of sight from the sidewalk, he stepped out of the shadow. They froze. He spoke calmly.

"Let me guess. Hopscotch tipped you that I was going to be at Octane and you followed me from there."

They did not bother denying it. They were all white men. One was blond, the other two had black hair. *Hired help?* They must have been. They moved like the kind of former soldiers often employed by private security companies. The cheap suits, faux-dress shoes with lugged soles, and ill-fitting overcoats screamed hired muscle.

Azriel knew Hopscotch had been acting odd. He made a mental note to have a nice little chat with the man. He continued, "So, now that we know how you found me, who sent you?"

The blond fellow in the middle spoke up.

"Our employer wants a word with you."

Azriel grinned. "A word? A word concerning what?"

The man replied, "She told us to bring you to her. That is the extent of the information we were given."

Azriel tilted his head, loosening his neck. Then he said, "I don't think that's going to work out for you. It would be better if you returned to your employer and told her you couldn't find me."

The blond man smirked and said, "Oh, you're coming with us, one way or another."

Just as the blond-haired thug stepped forward, a high, whining sound cut through the evening air. The black-haired goon to the blond fellow's right slumped to the ground with a grunt. When he fell forward, Azriel saw the knife sticking out of his back. Before he could shout a warning to the other two, they were all surrounded by men in black suits. These suits were much nicer. But, it was the red cloth tied around the biceps of their left arms that caught Azriel's attention. When he saw it, he immediately thought, *Asmodeus.* He looked over at the blond man and said, "Run. Now."

The man shook his head and replied, "Sorry, our employer warned us that if they came, we were supposed to protect you." Before Azriel could say anything more to man, he pulled his gun and fired. His remaining colleague did the same. The black-suited men swarmed around them like an angry, disturbed beehive. The bullets did not seem to affect any of them. The hired henchmen screamed as they were cut to shreds by the black-suited men wielding long, wickedly-curved, jewel-encrusted knives.

It wasn't until Azriel slashed one across the chest with his newly purchased knife that they reacted. The man he cut howled in pain as he spun away. The flesh around the cut sizzled. Even as the wounded man backpedaled, Azriel was among them. He twirled the knife in his hand, darting left and right. At what looked like six feet two or three on average, they were all a couple of inches taller than him – most were even heavier. But, Azriel stabbed, sliced, and cut, running through them like an obstacle course. They shrieked at the wounds inflicted by the ancient dagger. He broke through them, and headed for the street, slipping his dagger back into its sheath in his belt.

As he reached the sidewalk in front of Press and Grind, he heard five shots ring out. His back erupted in fire as three of the gunshots hit him. They spun him around before two more shots hit him in the chest. Had he not already sheathed his dagger, it would have tumbled from his hand. As he fell, he saw a woman on the sidewalk drop her coffee cup and pull a gun from the holster on her hip. She fired down the drive toward the acolytes. Azriel was out before he hit the ground.

He came awake with a start. It took a moment before Azriel realized he was being rocked gently, back and forth, like a baby in a sleeper. It took another moment to realize that it was the movement of a car. He was laying in the backseat. He sat up and said, "What is happening?"

The woman driving screamed, swerved the car, and then steered it back into the right lane, barely avoiding the oncoming traffic. She stared, wide-eyed, at Azriel in the rearview mirror, and said, "What *the* hell?! What. The. Hell. I thought you were dead. Wait, why aren't you dead? You were shot five times. You had no pulse. I checked. You were clearly dead. What the fuck is happening right now?!"

She pulled the car over, slamming on the breaks, and throwing it into park. With a shaky hand, she grabbed onto her gun, but she did not raise it. She just sat in the front staring over the seat at Azriel like he was a ghost.

After a few seconds, her eyes narrowed, and she said, "Goddammit. You better start talking or I will shoot you again, myself. The men who attacked you disappeared into the night after I put two of them down. When it was over, you were lying on the ground dead. Explain."

Azriel adjusted his shoulders, leaned back into the seat, and held up his hands in surrender. "Look, I know this all looks odd but I can explain. You are?"

The woman stared at him hard for another moment before taking her hand off her gun. She flipped open a black leather wallet revealing a shiny, gold badge on one side and a picture with a seal on the other. She said, "I'm Special Agent in Charge, Teresa Hernandez." Flipping her badge closed with a snap, she just stared at him. Her eyebrows were raised. Her lips were pursed. Everything about her expression said, *explain yourself.*

Azriel said, "It's very nice to meet you, Special Agent in Charge. And let me thank you for your help."

The agent shook her head and said, "Un uh, nope. I was not helping you. I stopped to grab a cup of coffee before heading back to the FBI field office over on Century when, suddenly, I started taking fire. I only saw you after I returned fire and those men in black suits faded into the night like something on fucking Netflix or the Syfy channel. I should still be there to meet the agents who are on their way to investigate the incident, but I needed to get you to a hospital, if for no other reason than to have you declared officially dead before I return to the scene. So, I'm going to ask you again, what the hell just happened, and why aren't you dead? In fact, while you're explaining that I had better get you to the hospital before you do die."

Azriel spoke calmly. "Agent Hernandez, that won't be necessary. I'm fine."

She blinked. "What do you mean, you're fine? You took three bullets to the back and two to the chest – specifically to the heart. You should be dead. Now, I'm trying to process why you aren't, and how you're just sitting there like fuck it, I'm good, but you're going to need to give me more than, I'm fine. The hell you are."

Azriel took off his jacket and shirt. He turned around and then back to face her so she could see. When he did, he heard her say, "What. The. Fuck!? Where are the bullet holes? You had five bullet holes in you. And they were all bleeding. Now all you have is dried blood on you? Un, uh. Nope. I'm not doing this. Not today."

Azriel said, "I understand this is all going to be hard to believe, but if you really want answers, drive me home. I'll explain everything when we get there."

Agent Hernandez stared at him for a while. Azriel saw the moment when curiosity beat out caution. It was a dark twinkle in her eyes. She turned back around and slowly placed her hands on the wheel. They were in a standard, black Charger, which likely had government plates.

While gazing out through the windshield onto the street ahead, she said, "Address. And when we get there you'd better start talking."

Azriel gave her his address. When she balked, he explained that, yes, it was in a commercial district, but it was where he lived. She pulled off into the night as he shrugged back into his bloodstained tee and jacket. The tee-shirt did not bother him. The three bullet holes in his leather jacket did. It was his favorite. He tried not to think about it as he rode in the backseat. It was not long before they were on his section of Atlanta Road. She pulled onto the lot, giving his building a visual once-over. She was probably trying to figure out what kind of business it housed. What was once a small parking lot out front was now a simple lawn of close-cut grass. The front door and windows were bricked in to make a solid wall. There was nothing about the front of the building that invited you to enter and he liked it that way.

"Pull around back, Special Agent."

Hernandez followed the blacktop driveway around to the back, while muttering something about, *in charge,* before parking in front of the garage door. Azriel waited for her to turn off the engine, step out, and open the back door for him. It was locked like a police car so that anyone in the back seat could not get out on their own. She popped the door open, while looking over his backyard. Her saw her note the landscaping, the tall, manicured hedges and the wooden fence preventing anyone on either side of his property, or behind it, from looking into his yard. A narrow, cut-rock path wove its way through the manicured bushes, small trees, and flower beds, to a small pavilion covered in matching stone, with iron-wrought chairs, and a table. It was all covered with a white trellis beneath a glass ceiling with iron legs holding it in the air.

Azriel stepped out of the car and said, “If you ask nicely, I’ll invite you back to sit over there and have a glass of bourbon with me.”

Hernandez chuckled, “I prefer vodka, on the rocks.”

He replied, “That can be arranged. My cellar is well-stocked.”

She turned from the yard, looked up at him, and said, “Hmph, I have no doubt.”

Azriel motioned to the only door in the exterior of the building. “This way, Special Agent Hernandez.”

With Hernandez in tow, he made his way to the purple door, covered by a second wrought-iron door. His key opened both, and he ushered her inside. Closing the doors behind him, he flipped on the light switch next to the door and pointed to one of the couches in his living room. “Make yourself at home while I change.” He turned to go, but then stopped and said, “Oh, may I please have my gun and knife back?”

Agent Hernandez looked at his outstretched hand with a quirked eyebrow. Azriel grinned, smiling wide, and said, “I wasn’t the one shooting at you, and we are in my home.”

She reached under her burgundy, leather jacket and pulled them out. She tossed him his knife and then his gun. Then, she placed all three of his magazines, and the round that had been in the chamber, on his coffee table. It did not escape Azriel's notice that while she was tossing him his weapons with her left hand, her right hovered casually near her right hip where her gun hung. A quick glance told him she was carrying a compact Sig Sauer P320.

He nodded toward her gun and said, "I thought the bureau went to Glock 9mm's recently. Why are you carrying a Sig?"

She was looking around his living room and over at his kitchen. He could see her Langley-trained mind cataloguing and assessing. She continued her mental inventory even as she said, "Well, aren't you perceptive. As a Special Agent in Charge, I have some leeway. Most agents can, if they desire, request to carry a firearm they choose as long as their superiors sign off, and the weapon meets certain criteria. We are still issued the Glock, and required to qualify on it. The overwhelming majority carry it. I just prefer my Sig."

Azriel nodded and headed for the stairs. "I'll be right back."

It did not take long for him to find a black tee, pull it on, and return to the living room. When he did, he found Hernandez sitting on the couch facing the door. He had no doubt it was a habit. He crossed the room and dropped onto the couch on the other side of the coffee table. Once he was comfortable, he produced a small knife he retrieved from his closet. When he did, he said, "Easy, Special Agent. This is how I explain to you what you saw this evening."

He could see her body shift. On the outside, she appeared calm and relaxed. But, he could tell she was ready to move in an instant. He kept the grin off his face and held up the knife with his right hand. He raised his left hand so that his palm faced her. A slight grimace accompanied the act of drawing the blade across his palm in a straight line. He still felt pain. The feel of the knife cutting into his skin was odd. Azriel kept his eyes on the woman as her expression changed from puzzled to awe. She watched the wound close up, right before her eyes. Finally, ignoring whatever potential threat she thought he might have posed, she leaped up off the couch, crossed the floor to where he sat, and grabbed his hand.

She ran her finger over the drying blood where the wound had been. Her eyes jumped from his palm to his face and back again. Her voice was a whisper, as she muttered, "That's not possible." It steadied as she continued, "If I hadn't seen you survive five bullets to the back and chest earlier Tonight, I would not believe what I'm seeing right now. Is this a trick? Do you think this is a game!?"

Azriel placed the knife on the coffee table, raised both of his hands and said, "I assure you Special Agent, this is not a game or a parlor trick. You simply stumbled into a world that most mortals live and die never having seen or known about."

He stood up and motioned for her to follow him. First, he stopped at the chessboard sitting next to the window in the living room. "I was given this chess set by Gerhardt Klausman himself, in 1862, after saving his daughter from what they called an Aushlick. It was a dark thing, set on keeping her in its basement to feed off. It lived on bodily fluid. I killed it and retrieved her. I wouldn't accept his money, so he gifted me one of the five sets he'd made."

Azriel moved on to a stand next to one of the tall bookshelves along the wall. The stand's upper half was a bodice on which hung an old fencing doublet. A sheathed saber leaned against the wall next to it. He pointed at them both, saying, "These are mementos from my time in the French Army in 1812 under Napoleon." He chuckled. "They came to call me the greatest swordsman in France. I had to prove that on several occasions."

Halfway up one of the other bookcases, he pointed out a six shooter in a glass case. It was a Smith & Wesson, Model 3, with a black grip and nickel finish. His voice dropped a bit as he said, "In 1870, I found my way to Arkansas. I was the first black U.S. Marshal west of the Mississippi. Just like every other time I had moved on to recreate myself and change my identity, before someone realized I wasn't getting any older, I did it in Arkansas. That was one of the times I lost myself in a life. It was hard to leave. I ignore the stories that came out of that time. They are always different from how things really were. In the legend, I'm a white man."

Azriel chuckled to himself again as he moved on to the far wall where a Gustav Klimt painting of a black woman in a starry nightgown hung. "In 1887, when I was in Vienna, I met a young, half-starving art student who'd just finished his studies at the Vienna School of Arts and Crafts known as the *Kunstgewerbeschule*. He was an interesting young man and we talked about art, poetry, and philosophy. Most days I paid for his meal, as he was apt to find me while I ate at a local café." Azriel shook his head at the memory while he stared at the masterpiece and its flaked-gold motif. "Shortly after his death, this arrived with a note from him, thanking me for my friendship, and keeping him from starving."

Hernandez looked at the painting and then over at him and said, "While I'm not an art buff, I've never seen this painting mentioned anywhere. I do know that the last Klimt's that sold at auction went for one hundred and thirty-two million dollars."

Azriel just kept walking without commenting on the worth of the painting. He made his way to a study of sorts at the end of the hallway on the first floor. It was spacious, with more bookshelves, an art deco table-desk with matching leather chair, and high ceilings. The floor was pale hardwood. A large, Persian rug covered much of the floor and sat under an Eames lounge chair and ottoman set covered in black leather with a walnut, wood shell. He stopped at the katana and matching wakizashi perched on a black stand, covered in purple silk, against the far wall. They were identical accept in length. The scabbards, called *saya*, were rust-colored with gold medallions painted down their length at equal intervals. The round handguards, or *tsubas,* were golden. The hilts, known as *tsuka*, were wrapped in brown silk revealing the white rayskin covering the hilt beneath the wrap. The cord, called *sageo*, made of heavy silk, like flat rope, was wrapped, intricately, around the upper part of the scabbard. It was white with a pattern of burgundy dots covering it.

"These are from my time in Japan. In 1581, I served under the Hegemon and warlord, Oda Nobunaga. I rose to the rank of samurai. I was the only black man who ever had. As a gift, on the day I attained the title, Lord Nobunaga presented me with this katana and wakizashi. I protected him until the day he died. He was an honorable man. I left Japan and I've never been back."

Azriel turned and directed Hernandez to the set of chairs bracketing a small table in his study. They sat, and he continued, "I could go on showing you the things I've picked up on my travels or describing the lives I've lived. I keep the mementos because they are the markers of my journey through time. I'm what we call the *Long-lived* – one of the immortals who walk the earth."

Special Agent Hernandez looked at him and then at the Japanese swords. When she returned her gaze to him, exasperated, she just said, "How?"

Azriel took a deep breath and sighed, before saying, “It’s a story of shame. A shame that I’ve been trying to atone for, for the last two thousand years.” He saw her flinch at the number. He continued, “Yes, two thousand years, give or take a decade. You see, those of us who are immortal, have come to it in different ways. Vlad was a necromancer. He used dark magic and an agreement with Old Scratch himself to become immortal. More specifically, and this is important – he was made *undead.* Never make a deal with the Scion of Hell.”

Azriel leaned back in his chair as he warmed to the subject. “Magnus Salford found an elixir in an ancient cave in Ethiopia while working at an archeological dig. The fool drank it. Galen Verille Du Loc was punished by a Romani Magi after burning the camp she and her traveling tribe set up, in an effort to chase them off his property. He howls at the full moon in regret. And I? My shame is the greatest.”

They sat there in silence for a few more heartbeats. Hernandez looked at him like she did not believe a word of it, but then, like she knew it was all true. The sound of glass breaking interrupted them. Azriel was moving before Hernandez knew what was happening. *How had they found him,* he wondered? He stopped halfway to the door of his office and turned around. Hernandez ran right into him. He was running his hands over her before she even realized what was happening. When she opened her mouth, likely to complain about his hands, he showed her the tiny, black tracker – its red dot blinking – he pulled from under the collar of her leather jacket. First, she grimaced, and then she dropped her head forward.

She muttered under her breath, "Are you a rookie?" The frustrated tone of the question made it clear that it was rhetorical and aimed at herself. She pulled her gun from her holster. Azriel heard the soft click of the safety being removed while he pulled the ancient katana free from its scabbard. Somehow, during whatever scuffle had ensued while he was passed out, one of the acolytes managed to place a tracker on her hoping it would lead them to Azriel. They were right.

He saw the look of disgust on her face. There was no need to rub it in. So, he just shrugged his shoulders at her. Then, with a twirl of the sword in his right hand, he floated down the hallway toward the living room. Azriel knew exactly who he was going to find. There was no residual smell of an explosive device. There had been no sound prior to the shattering of glass. Given, that his windows were three-and-a-half-inch ballistic glass, it would have taken a tremendous amount of force to break them. So, when he rounded the corner, with Hernandez covering his left flank, he was not surprised to see Asmodeus sitting in a chair surrounded by glass and twelve of his hulking acolytes. To her credit, Hernandez did not flinch. She just trained her gun on the man in the chair.

Azriel rose from his slight crouch, lowering his sword to his side. He made a show of looking around at the broken glass littering his living room floor. When he turned back to look at a smug Asmodeus, lounging in the wide, oversized, white, leather chair between the two couches, Azriel simply said, "Really?"

Asmodeus was tall, slim, and wrapped in a black, three-piece suit, tailored to within an inch of its life. A crisp, white, French-cuffed shirt gleamed from under the black wool. A thin, black, silk tie jutted from his neck before curling down under the vest. Diamonds glittered from the white-gold cufflinks, and the heavy, eighteen million-dollar Jacob and Company watch on his wrist. He had good taste, even if it was decadent. The watch was known as the billionaire watch and came with two hundred and sixty carats of emerald-cut diamonds. His thin, pale hands boasted manicured finger nails coated with a clear polish that glistened in the soft light. The black, patent leather oxfords were accented with suede across the uppers where they laced. If he knew Asmodeus they were Italian - likely TesTony. His black hair was short at the sides, but longer, with a bit of fuss, across the front, and coated with gel. He was old school, so he was clean-shaven. While he looked like a man of about forty, he was a demon, and one of the oldest of his kind – like a prince in a kingdom of hellspawn. He unbuttoned his jacket, crossed one leg over the other, and smiled a smile that was so full of itself Azriel felt greasy just looking at it.

His voice was twice as slick as his smile. "Come, come now, my good man. Have a seat. We have so much to discuss."

Azriel looked around at the acolytes. They were Half-men. Men seduced by whatever Asmodeus had promised – wealth, power, sex – all the usual enticements – and then given dark power in order to serve their master. Whatever was done to them had changed them, though. They were not demons, but they were not simply men anymore either.

Asmodeus clucked, “Ah, ah, ah. Now, stay calm. I know you’re immortal, thanks to that meddlesome freak of nature these glorified monkeys worship. But, I don’t need to kill you to make you suffer. For example, I could have my acolytes cut you into several pieces and put them in boxes to be buried all over the world. Your head in one place, your arms and legs in another? You get the idea. Now, sit the fuck down!” Spittle clung to his thin lips as he tried to reign in his temper. Azriel had always had that effect on him.

Azriel said, “Let the woman go, Asmodeus. She’s a Special Agent of the FBI. If she goes missing, it will bring all kinds of unwanted attention down on your head. While that might not affect you directly, it will definitely put a crimp in your plans.”

Asmodeus looked over at Hernandez as though considering Azriel’s request, but before the demon could answer, Hernandez blurted, “I’m not going anywhere. These assholes took a shot at me, and planted a tracker on me. You don’t do either of those without getting my full attention.”

Asmodeus clapped his hands loudly. "Yes, yes! I like her. Well said, Agent Hernandez."

Hernandez barked, "That's Special Agent in Charge, to you."

Asmodeus leaned forward in the chair, cackling with a giddiness Azriel did not like one bit. He replied, "Oh, I really, really like her. You know, Azriel, after you and I settle a few things, I'm going to have a little bit of fun with *Special Agent in Charge* Hernandez." He looked at Hernandez like she was a fresh meal placed on the table in front of him and said, *"Te voy a dar una noche que nunca te vas a olvidar, eh chica."*

Hernandez blanched, and swallowed hard, but her gun did not waiver. Her only response was to turn up her lip in revulsion. Azriel's jaw clenched, and his hand tightened on the hilt of his sword. Asmodeus turned back to him and said, "Now, where were we? Oh, yes. We were about to discuss that item you stole from me in Mesopotamia. And how no one steals from me and gets away with it. How long has it been? Three hundred years? You've been a hard man to find. I especially want to know what little totem or trick you've been using to keep yourself hidden from me. I actually had to break down and use the conventional means these walking apes use to find each other. It took forever. And low and behold, you're hiding in Atlanta of all places."

Asmodeus stood up and continued, "Well, let's get to it, shall we? Acolytes, take the woman to the car and restrain Azriel."

Everything in the room slowed down. The air got heavy. It only took a second for Azriel to realize it was not a mental trick borne out of being in a high-pressure situation. It was real. He went to raise his sword but his hand moved like it weighed a ton. Three of the acolytes slowly burst into green flames like a movie scene running in slow motion. Three more went flying through the air at what must have been an inch a second. In the middle of it all, a woman came strolling through the broken window behind them. She was tall, with thick braids of black hair woven close to her scalp and falling down her back to her waist. Her skin was dark brown. She had a small ring of gold medallions strung across her forehead on a chain like a tiara. Her full lips were painted black. High cheek bones and a strong chin, complemented big brown eyes, and a medium-sized nose. She was perfect. Her arms and legs were muscular without being bulky. The gown was sheer, with fitted sleeves, and a plunging neckline. It hugged her body and split up the front so that it revealed her legs up to her thighs as she walked. The split skirt was so long it trailed the ground behind her. The sleeves, chest, bodice, and skirt were covered in red, flowery embroidery. She was perched on four-inch heels. The shoes had a wide strap around the ankle, and one across the front of her foot, with a gold buckle on the end, showing toes painted with the same black polish as coated her long fingernails. A gold choker encircled her neck, glistening with diamonds and rubies, matching a thick bracelet, and several rings on her fingers. Her lithe fingers were adorned with long, armor rings, complemented by thinner rings nestled above and below her knuckles. When she reached the center of the room everything sped back up to normal speed. The acolytes on fire dissolved into small heaps of ash. The three that were drifting through the air, slammed into the wall and then dropped to the floor with a loud crack.

Freed from the effects of whatever had slowed them, one of Asmodeus' acolytes rushed the woman. He was large, burly, and a full foot taller than her. But, she just reached out and grabbed him by the neck as he reached for her, hoisting him into the air like she was picking up her car keys. She watched him kick and choke as she held him a few feet off the ground and squeezed. When he stopped moving, she dropped him like he was an empty coffee cup being thrown into a garbage can – his face was purple, his tongue hung out of his mouth. As he hit the ground, she tipped over the broken glass, crossing the room to where Azriel was now standing. It was like watching a model on a Paris Fashion Week runway. She was glorious.

Standing on those heels she was just as tall as he was. When she reached him, she grabbed the sides of his face in her hands and kissed him on the lips like a long, lost lover. When she finished, she leaned back, looked at his face, and rubbed her lipstick off his lips with her right thumb. Then, she smiled at him with perfect, white teeth, and said, "Hello, darling. How are you? You've been a very naughty boy. You know I've been looking for you.

Why did you run away from my men? I know they look pedestrian, but that old saying is still true – good help is hard to find." She glanced around the room at Asmodeus' acolytes and continued, "Besides, you know I'm not really into henchmen. It's so – 'I want to rule the world-ish.' And I have more important things to do with my time."

Azriel cleared his throat before replying, "Hello, Lilith. It's good to see you, especially under these circumstances. But, I didn't go with your hired thugs because I haven't changed my mind since the last time we spoke."

Lilith straightened herself. Rising to her full height, she put her hands on her hips, and said, "Hmph." Then, she waved away what Azriel had just said, like it never happened. Turning to look at Hernandez, she spoke with a strong undercurrent of displeasure in her voice. "Don't be rude, lover. Introduce me to your friend."

He said, "Lilith, this is Special Agent in Charge, Teresa Hernandez. Agent Hernandez, this is Lilith."

Lilith stepped over to Hernandez and stuck out her hand, with a wicked smile on her face. Hernandez glanced over at Azriel and then back at her. With a half-smile painting her own face, she lowered her gun before reaching out to shake Lilith's hand. When Lilith released the woman's hand after pumping her arm a few times, she said, "And what designs, may I ask, do you have on this handsome immortal?"

Hernandez's mouth fell open. She looked like she was stuck. Lilith said, "Oh, don't be shy, my dear. I understand. He's a lovely piece of yum-yum. But, he plays hard to get."

Before Hernandez could collect her wits enough to respond, Lilith was already turning to face Asmodeus. "Take a moment to get yourself together Special Agent in Charge, we have other things to deal with in the meantime."

Azriel had never seen Asmodeus look like he wanted to crawl under a rock. The demon looked around as if he was contemplating running, or at least trying to. Instead, he quickly dropped to a knee. His voice was full of reverence as he said, "My Lady, it is an honor to be in your presence. Please understand that I mean no disrespect, but I have business with the Wanderer."

Hernandez blurted out, "Wait, she's the Lilith from the Bible. The first wife of Adam, before Eve?"

The lights dimmed. Lilith moved faster than even Azriel could see. In a blink, she was back in Hernandez' face, but this time she was so close that only a hairsbreadth separated them. Lilith's mouth opened in an inhuman shriek of rage. For the first time, her fangs were visible. Hernandez had closed her eyes as if she was waiting for the end to come at any second. Her hands trembled as they clutched her gun in a tight grip at her waist.

Azriel spoke calmly as Lilith hovered there. "No, Agent Hernandez. Most everything written about Lilith was written by men interested in the subjugation of women. She became the embodiment of the hysterical, evil woman, the mother of demons, who needed to be controlled. Rather than portray her in her true light, as the equal of men, they painted her as a rebellious spirit – a warning to other women through the ages to stay in their place."

As he spoke, he slowly moved over to where Lilith stood in front of Hernandez. "The truth is, she was the first creation. A creature of celestial beauty and power. A being of light, meant as a guardian of the creatures that were to come after her. But, men rejected that protection. And so, she left them to their downfall and destruction."

Lilith turned her head to look at Azriel and said, "Flatterer."

He smiled at her, took her hand, and twirled her as if they were dancing. The light in the room brightened, and he swayed back and forth with her until she giggled like a little girl. He looked in her eyes and said, "You are the most beautiful woman I have ever known."

Lilith stopped and pushed him back saying, "Don't worry, I'm not going to hurt your little Special Agent."

Turning her attention back to Asmodeus, who had begun to quietly tip out through the broken window, she clucked her tongue and said, "Ah, ah, ah. Where do you think you're going?"

Asmodeus stopped and turned back to face her. "My Lady, I thought I would leave you to your business."

Lilith waved a hand and the rest of Asmodeus' acolytes went up in green flames. The howls were blood curdling, and the smell was awful. In seconds, they were ash. Asmodeus' shoulders slumped, but his eyes narrowed. Lilith said, "Don't worry, I'm not going to interfere with what you came here to do. I'm just making it a fair fight."

Azriel was moving even as Lilith finished. The woman's motives had always been difficult to discern. You could never really know what she was going to do until she did it. He threw the sword at the demon as he leaped over the table. Asmodeus batted it out of the way. But, before he could do anything else, Azriel was on him. He grabbed him by his neck with both hands and said, "Emesza Ka Procume!"

Asmodeus screamed as his neck burned where Azriel's hands encircled it. He hit Azriel with a backhand blow that sent him flying over the couch. Azriel hit the ground hard but rolled up onto his feet in a blink. As he got to his feet, Asmodeus reached out a hand toward him. A burst of red light engulfed Azriel, but quickly faded. Lilith laughed out loud. Azriel felt his necklace warm as its charm of protection quenched the demon fire. He leaped back over the couch tackling Asmodeus to the floor. He grabbed the demon's face with his left hand, which held his ring and shouted, "Xai Mos!"

His hand glowed bright-white. Asmodeus howled. The ancient thing was strong. Even under the compulsion of a talisman of light, he pushed Azriel's hand, slowly, away from his face. A knee to Azriel's stomach threw him off the demon. The dark creature was on his feet in an instant. Azriel leaped up to his own. The ring had left the mark of the Eye of Heru on the side of Asmodeus' face. It was red, angry looking, and still had smoke coming off it. Asmodeus looked from Lilith to Azriel and said, "Another time, Wanderer." With a wave of his arm, Asmodeus disappeared in a thick swirl of black, acrid smoke, leaving the room smelling of sulfur.

Azriel walked over to the broken window and looked out on the night. Everything was suddenly, oddly, quiet. Behind him, Lilith clapped her hands as if she had just finished watching an orchestra perform on an opera stage.

"That was extremely entertaining, darling. If I were you, I'd find that creature and put an end to him before he finds you again. I'd hate to have to stop what I'm doing to try and find all the little boxes he'd buried you in."

Lilith sauntered over to where he was standing. He could not stop his heart from clenching at how stunning she was. As if she could hear his thoughts, she smiled a long, languid smile and said, "Me too, lover. Me too." She kissed him, lightly, on his cheek, like a tiny bird alighting on a thin branch.

Whispering in his ear, she said, "Until next time, lover. Since your hands are full at the moment, we can discuss why I'm in Atlanta in a few days. Until then, have fun."

Turning to Hernandez, Lilith said, "You can have him for now, darling. But, in the end, remember, he belongs to me."

With that, she stepped through the window and disappeared into the night, leaving Hernandez sputtering.

"Tell that woman that I … You let her know that we … You need to make it clear to that woman that …". After a moment, she gave up. Shoving her gun back into her holster, she said, "I don't even know how to process what just happened. I can't write any of this in a report or I'll lose my badge and end up in some mental facility on heavy drugs."

Azriel just sat on the couch and let her process. After a few minutes, she said, "I'm going to go back to the scene at the Press and Grind and say something about a robbery gone wrong and a missing victim that no one can identify."

She started toward the broken window, stopped, thought better of it and turned toward the door they had entered. When she got to the door she turned around, looked at Azriel, and said, "So, you really are immortal. And there's a whole world filled with people like you?"

Azriel nodded, raised his eyebrows, and said, "Yes. I was passing through Jerusalem during the holy week of Passover. I stopped on a road where a crowd was gathered. The Roman soldiers were busy preparing a man for their butcher's rite, called crucifixion, reserved for criminals, but meant to send a message. It was brutal and often effective. To my everlasting shame, I joined in on the heckling. They were forcing a man to carry his own cross up to the hill where they would complete the horrendous deed. And because I was a small man, swayed by the mob, I joined in. I shouted insults at him. For some reason, he stopped. I shouted again, asking him what was he waiting for? And it was like mine was the only voice he heard through the cacophony all around us. He looked up and stared right into my eyes. And then, he spoke."

Standing at the door, Hernandez crossed herself, starting at her forehead and ending across her chest as if to ward off an evil spirit. Her voice trembled as she said, "What did he say?"

Azriel continued, "His eyes pierced me like a cold knife to the heart. And he said, *I shall stand and rest, but you will go on until the Last Day.* And when he said it, I knew it was true. He'd cursed me to never die, until the world comes to an end. From then on, they called me the Wanderer."

Teresa Hernandez stood at his door for a moment more, nodding her head almost imperceptibly, before saying, "I need a drink."

She opened the door to leave and stopped. "What if I run into something from your world again?"

Azriel smiled and said, "You know where to find me."

Hernandez left, closing the door behind her. Azriel looked around at the mess that was his living room. There was a number he could call to have it all cleaned up as if it never happened. It was not the first time his world attempted to burst through to the world of mortals. But first, he needed to get his car. He opened the app on his phone that would route a car to his address to give him a ride back to Virginia Street and marveled at how the world had changed in the last two thousand years. Then, he went upstairs to get his other leather jacket.

Terminus Authors
(in alphabetical order)

Gerald Coleman (The Messiah Curse)

Gerald L. Coleman is a Philosopher, Theologian, Poet, and Author residing in Atlanta. Born in Lexington, he did his undergraduate work in Philosophy and English at the University of Kentucky. He followed that by completing a degree in Religious Studies and concluding with a Master's degree in Theology at Trevecca Nazarene University in Nashville. His most recent poetry appears in, Pluck! The Journal of Affrilachian Arts & Culture, Drawn To Marvel: Poems From The Comic Books, Pine Mountain Sand & Gravel Vol. 18, Black Bone Anthology, the 10th Anniversary Issue of Diode Poetry Journal, and About Place Journal. He is a speculative fiction author with short stories published in the Science Fiction, Cyberfunk Anthology: *The City,* the Rococoa Anthology by Roaring Lion, and the upcoming Dark Universe and Terminus Urban Fantasy Anthology. He is the author of the Epic Fantasy novel saga *The Three Gifts,* which currently includes *When Night Falls* (Book One) and *A Plague of Shadows* (Book Two).

He has appeared on panels at DragonCon, SOBSFCon, Atlanta Science Fiction & Fantasy Expo, and has been a Guest Author and panelist at JordonCon, The Outer Dark Symposium, Imaginarium Con, and Boskone. He is a co-founder of the Affrilachian Poets and has recently released three collections of poetry entitled *the road is long, falling to earth,* and *microphone check.* You can find him at geraldlcoleman.co.

Milton Davis (Piggyback)

Milton Davis is a Black Speculative fiction writer and owner of MVmedia, LLC, a small publishing company specializing in Science Fiction, Fantasy and Sword and Soul. MVmedia's mission is to provide speculative fiction books that represent people of color in a positive manner. Milton is the author of seventeen novels; his most recent is the Sword and Soul adventure *Son of Mfumu*. He is the editor and co-editor of seven anthologies; *The City, Dark Universe* with Gene Peterson; *Griots*: *A Sword and Soul Anthology and Griot: Sisters of the Spear*, with Charles R. Saunders; *The Ki Khanga Anthology,* the *Steamfunk! Anthology*, and the *Dieselfunk anthology* with Balogun Ojetade. MVmedia has also published *Once Upon A Time in Afrika* by Balogun Ojetade and *Abegoni: First Calling* and *Nyumbani Tales* by Sword and Soul creator and icon Charles R. Saunders. Milton's work had also been featured in *Black Power: The Superhero Anthology*; Skelos *2: The Journal of*

Weird Fiction and Dark Fantasy Volume 2, *Steampunk Writes Around the World* published by Luna Press and *Bass Reeves Frontier Marshal Volume Two*.

M. Haynes (Not Your (Magical) Negro)

M. Haynes' childhood was so filled with fantasy worlds that he just had to create one of his own. This Memphis-born, Mississippi-bred son of the South was inspired all through his upbringing by books like Harry Potter and Animorphs, TV shows like Avatar the Last Airbender, and video games like Legend of Dragoon to start writing, a passion he has continued to adulthood. His YA science fantasy the Elemental series and his other writings take a different turn from most of his childhood fantasy worlds, however. Armed with over fifteen years of writing experience, M. Haynes has set out to produce works that show that you don't have to be a straight, blonde haired, blue eyed guy to be a superhero. Instead, he hopes to show a more nuanced version of people of color in fantasy worlds, maybe even encouraging young P.O.C. to love reading and writing as he does. You can learn more about M. Haynes and his work at www.mhaynes.org/elemental.

Alan Jones (Blerd and Confused)

Amazon Best-selling author & former Wall Street consultant, Alan Jones was born and raised in Atlanta,

GA. He has three Sci-Fi books under his belt, *To Wrestle with Darkness, Sacrifices* and his latest, *Heretics*. Alan has also contributed to a number of Anthologies, such as "The City: A *CyberFunk Anthology*", *Possibilities*& the soon to be released *Terminus*. Alan was formerly a columnist with the Atlanta Tribune, as well being a movie reviewer for *The Technique* & *The Signal* during his college days. When not writing, Alan works as an Oracle Consultant.

Alan attended Georgia Tech and the Robinson School of Business, obtaining his MBA from the latter. www.Alandjones.com

Kyoko M (My Dinner with Vlad)

Kyoko M is a USA Today bestselling author, a fangirl, and an avid book reader. She has a Bachelor of Arts in English Lit degree from the University of Georgia, which gave her every valid excuse to devour book after book with a concentration in Greek mythology and Christian mythology. When not working feverishly on a manuscript (or two), she can be found buried under her Dashboard on Tumblr, or chatting with fellow nerds on Twitter, or curled up with a good Harry Dresden novel on a warm Georgia night. Like any author, she wants nothing more than to contribute something great to the best profession in the world, no matter how small.

Violette Meier (Another Day in the A)

Violette Meier is a happily married mother, writer, painter, poet, and native of Atlanta, Georgia, who earned my B.A. in English at Clark Atlanta University and a Masters of Divinity at Interdenominational Theological Center.

Her books include: *The First Chronicle of Zayashariya: Out of Night*, *Angel Crush*, *Son of the Rock*, *Tales of a Numinous Nature: A Short Story Collection*, *Violette Ardor: A Volume of Poetry,* and *This Sickness We Call Love: Poems of Love, Lust, and Lamentation*, *Ruah the Immortal,* and *Loving and Living Life* are now available.

Balogun Ojetade (Bomani and the Case of the Missing Monsters)

As Technical Director of the Afrikan Martial Arts Institute and Co-Chair of the Urban Survival and Preparedness Institute, Balogun Ojetade is the author of the bestselling non-fiction books *Afrikan Martial Arts: Discovering the Warrior Within*, *The Afrikan Warriors Bible*, *Surviving the Urban Apocalypse*, *The Urban Self Defense Manual*, *The Young Afrikan Warriors' Guide to Defeating Bullies & Trolls*, *Never Unarmed: The Afrikan Warriors' Guide to Improvised Weapons*, *Ofo Ase: 365 Daily Affirmations to Awaken the Afrikan Warrior Within*, *Ori: The Afrikan Warriors' Mindset* and *Ogun Ye! Protecting the Afrikan Family and Community.*

He is one of the leading authorities on Afroretroism – film, fashion or fiction that combines African and / or African American culture with a blend of "retro" styles and futuristic technology, in order to explore the themes of tension between past and future and between the alienating and empowering effects of technology and on Creative Resistance. He writes about Afroretroism – Sword & Soul, Rococoa, Steamfunk and Dieselfunk at http://chroniclesofharriet.com/.

He is author of eighteen novels and gamebooks – *MOSES: The Chronicles of Harriet Tubman (Books 1 & 2)*; *The Chronicles of Harriet Tubman: Freedonia*; *Redeemer*; *Once Upon A Time In Afrika*; *Fist of Afrika*; *A Single Link*; *Wrath of the Siafu*; *The Scythe*; *The Keys*; *Redeemer: The Cross Chronicles*; *Beneath the Shining Jewel*; *Q-T-Pies: The Savannah Swan Files (Book 0)* and *A Haunting in the SWATS: The Savannah Swan Files (Book 1)*; *Siafu Saves the World*; *Siafu vs. The Horde; Dembo's Ditty*; and *The Beatdown* – contributing co-editor of three anthologies: *Ki: Khanga: The Anthology*, *Steamfunk* and *Dieselfunk* and contributing editor of the *Rococoa* anthology and *Black Power: The Superhero Anthology*.

He is also the creator and author of the Afrofuturistic manga series, *Jagunjagun Lewa (Pretty Warrior)* and co-author of the *Ngolo* graphic novel.

Finally, he is co-author of the award winning screenplay, *Ngolo* and co-creator of *Ki Khanga: The Sword and Soul*

Role-Playing Game, both with author Milton Davis.

.

Aziza Sphinx (Play the Wraith)

Aziza Sphinx is a firm believer that reading and writing go hand and hand. A Southerner through and through, she loves her peaches and pecans while curling up with a good book. A master of resourcefulness, her love of research leads her down paths of discovery that touch every aspect of her writing. Her love of reading ignited her passion for writing, leading her to frequently fill page after page with tales of her beloved characters' adventures. She loves to sprinkle facts about her beloved Georgia throughout her fictional worlds as an influence and an adversary.

Kortney Y. Watkins (Of Home and Hearth)

Kortney Y. Watkins is a poet, short-story writer, novelist, and educator. She lives for love, waits on the moon, and hopes for the sake of humanity; every slash of a pen and stroke of a key is dedicated to exploring those things often done, less considered. She resides in the Atlanta metropolitan area amongst loving kin and friends.

CPSIA information can be obtained
at www.ICGtesting.com
Printed in the USA
LVHW03s2318150618
580966LV00001B/19/P